Underlying Love A Worthington, Ohio Mystery

Underlying Love, Volume 1

Bradley Barkhurst

Published by Bradley Barkhurst, 2024.

This is a work of fiction. Similarities to real people, places, or events are entirely coincidental.

UNDERLYING LOVE A WORTHINGTON, OHIO MYSTERY

First edition. June 16, 2024.

ISBN: 979-8227362162

Written by Bradley Barkhurst.

Table of Contents

This book is dedicated to Don O'Brien whose photographs helped preserve Worthington's 1940s history.

Even though this story and characters are fictional, several businesses and places Don photographed are in the story.

Also, thank you to my mother for editing this novel and being a great mom! Finally, thank you to my father, who was president of the Old Worthington Association and instilled in me a curiosity about Worthington's history. Thanks, Dad!

Finally, please stop by www.underlyinglove.com for Underlying Love merch, news, and free gifts!

Chapter 1: Cracks Beneath the Surface

The morning sun peeked over the rooftops of the Village of Worthington, Ohio, ushering in the start of another day. As the sounds of the Worthington Presbyterian Church bells rang at eight, echoing down High Street, shopkeepers began turning store signs from closed to open. Displays of fresh produce and hand-lettered signs beckoned customers strolling the sidewalks.

The Village of Worthington was coming back to life after years of hardship. It was now September 1941 and the worst of the Great Depression had passed, though its specter still loomed. Most of the Worthington businesses along High Street and Granville Road had survived the lean years. The busy Home Market, Ault Hardware, and the Worthington Savings Bank welcomed familiar faces each morning.

Further south, at the corner of High Street and West New England Avenue, stood the stately New England Inn, a landmark since 1816 built by Rensselear W. Cowles for $250. The village had transformed around it for over a century. After a fire in 1901, the inn was renovated to include a lavish ballroom and balcony on the third floor. Well-dressed travelers motioned bellhops to collect their luggage from freshly polished sedans.

In the middle of the village, was the jewel of Worthington - the Village Green, a sprawling 3.5-acre commons divided into quadrants running between High Street and Granville Road. Originally it was set aside by the village's founding fathers in 1803 for livestock grazing.

Now it was spruced with tall trees ranging from the Ohio Buckeye to the American Sweetgum. Passing through the trees were footpaths crisscrossed throughout the green. It was the showcase of Worthington and home to the annual summer ice cream social and the Christmas tree lighting ceremony.

On this morning, Elizabeth Russo was walking down her driveway to walk to school. The cheerfulness of the villagers was always shining through.

Clotheslines fluttered between houses up and down nearby streets, the day's laundry drying in the gentle breeze. Betty Whimsfeld, Elizabeth's next-door neighbor, hummed to herself as she pinned up two of her deceased husband's large dress shirts, using them as makeshift curtains in her front room. Eccentric but good-natured, Betty and her unconventional projects were a common sight around the neighborhood.

"Good morning, Elizabeth!" Betty chimed. "Off to school now?"

"Yes Betty, I'm off to see the boys and girls!" Elizabeth said.

"Well, have a wonderful day!" said Betty.

"I will, thank you, Betty!" Elizbeth excitedly replied.

As she walked onto High Street, Police Officer Jameson whistled a tune while making his usual rounds.

"Good morning, Miss Russo!" Officer Jameson said as he saw Elizabeth approaching.

"Good morning, Officer Jameson, beautiful day this morning!" Elizabeth gleefully replied.

He tipped his cap to the residents, offered a nickel to a shoeshine boy, and reminded some high schoolers not to roller skate on the sidewalks. His genial presence added to the village's welcoming charm.

Nearby, Mr. McFoley parked his mail truck in its usual spot. The postal carrier had been delivering letters to Worthington residents for over two decades with great pride. His leather satchel was overstuffed with postcards, letters, and magazines. As he began his route down

High Street on foot, Mr. McFoley mentally noted which mailer each customer would want to read first.

"Morning Elizabeth, on the way to school, are ya?" greeted Mr. McFoley.

"Indeed, I am Mr. McFoley." said Elizabeth.

"Well tell those kiddos, Postman McFoley hopes they study hard."

"I will, Mr. McFoley." said Elizabeth, nodding her head.

On the outskirts of the village sat the small train stop, Worthington Station, which was still bustling with activity. A few freight cars waited to be loaded with grain and livestock from local farms headed to Cincinnati. People had started to line up ready to commute to work on the passenger train to downtown Columbus. The distant whistles of approaching trains announced brief stops in Worthington before continuing southward to the Ohio River.

Across the tracks was the Potter Lumber and Supply Company, a hardwood supplier for the central Ohio area. Next to the station, stood a small cluster of ramshackle houses, no longer maintained. This is where Hobo Jeff lay passed out in a drunken stupor. The disheveled man survived on odd jobs and the charity of kind souls. For the most part, the village accepted him as part of life in Worthington.

Elizabeth Gracie Russo loved her community. She had grown up exploring every street and wooded trail from the Jeffers Indian Mound to the Olentangy River. As an only child, her father, a Sicilian immigrant, would bring her along to chat with shopkeepers. Now at 23, Elizabeth was one of the fortunate ones. She worked hard through school to become an elementary teacher. Her father, who had struggled for years as an immigrant, always found a way to make money allowing his daughter to live a comfortable life. By the time she was in high school, Elizabeth was already wearing chic clothing.

Elizabeth was blessed with natural Sicilian beauty. She had an elegant figure that turned the heads of men when she strolled by. Her dark, wavy hair cascaded just past her shoulders, and she had a heart-shaped face with delicate features. When she smiled, it lit up the entire room with a warmth that put even the shyest children at ease. She often wore just a touch of rouge on her defined cheekbones and a dab of red lipstick that accentuated her classy look.

Worthington was still a place where neighbors looked out for one another. Most residents of the village were humble, honest people, but society was fraying a bit at the edges. Elizabeth noticed more vagrants near the station, despair etched on their faces as they waited for the next train heading...anywhere. Some families had lost their houses and moved, never to return. Even those who stayed changed in subtle ways. Laughter didn't come quite as easily. Jaws remained clenched. The Great Depression had whispered a truth - nothing was promised, no matter how hard one worked.

Still, familiarity and routine offered comfort. As Elizabeth walked further up High Street, the scent of Miss Lilah's freshly baked bread at the Home Market brought a smile to her face. Taking in the fresh morning air she felt alive.

She saw Old Man Kendrick shuffling down High Street to his usual bench. Worthington was home, even if home wasn't quite the sanctuary it once had been. Its streets were filled with memories and meaning, even if a bit faded by hardship.

"Good morning, Elizabeth. You're looking young and vibrant this morning." Mr. Kendrick said sitting from his bench.

"You too Mr. Kendrick." winked Elizabeth as she passed by.

As the 1940s dawned, the discussion was about a war half a world away. But for now, Worthington clung to normalcy - mail delivered, streets policed, little moments shared as they had been for decades. Storefront windows welcomed customers as best they could, hopeful that this decade might bring renewal.

Elizabeth took pride in being part of such a close-knit community. She knew almost everyone in the village after growing up just down the street from the Worthington School at 50 East Granville Road, where she taught. Familiar faces were everywhere – the Worthington Savings Bank manager who still slipped her cookies, the Brown Fruit Farm that would deliver apples and pumpkins in the fall. There was comfort in having roots planted firmly.

One fixture of the village was the modest Red and White general store on High Street just south of the Village Green. It used to be run by Elizabeth's father. The worn wooden floors and creaky shelves stocked with flour sacks and cracker barrels were a second home to her as a child. Neighbors would stop in for tobacco or canned goods while sharing the latest village gossip. During busy harvest times, local farmers gathered out front to talk about the weather and crops before loading up feed bags and supplies. It was always welcoming with a "Have A Coke" sign outside. Elizabeth waved to employees through the window as she passed by.

After her father's passing, two years prior, keeping the store open became Elizabeth's silent mission. There had been more competition moving in, such as Kroger's grocery store, making it harder to compete. She had to take out a loan from Worthington Savings Bank to keep stocked. Each well-worn surface and aging sign felt like a living relic of her dad. Fortunately, running the store wasn't so difficult with the help of her father's former assistant, now store manager, John. He helped hire a few employees who were responsible for the store's daily operations. Elizabeth didn't know how she could keep the place open without him. The store had become infused with nostalgia. Sitting at the counter on quiet weekend afternoons made her feel her father's comforting presence for a fleeting moment.

Elizabeth had warm memories of her father, though his death still haunted her. He passed away while driving to Columbus to get supplies for the store. He swerved the car to miss a drunk who had suddenly walked into the street. His car crashed into a truck going in the opposite direction. Onlookers said it happened so quickly that he probably didn't know what happened. With him gone, Elizabeth did her best to focus on the future.

In truth, though, she found herself clinging more to the past. She reflected on memories of not only her father but her high school sweetheart, Samuel Lewis, who had to leave the village during the Great Depression. With him gone, the years felt so uncertain, like a candle whose glow could be extinguished by the slightest wind.

Better to focus on the tasks at hand - teaching the next generation, keeping the store in order, and playing her part in the community. She went through the familiar motions, steadying herself against waves of restlessness and longing that arose at odd moments. There was comfort in repetition and purpose. Undeniably, though, she felt an undercurrent just below the surface of unease these days.

As she walked in, morning light filtered into the school as Elizabeth prepared for another day. She neatly arranged the small wooden desks, lightly polishing nicks and scratches etched by restless students. Opening the windows, she welcomed in the soothing autumn birdsong – a brief break before young voices would fill the room.

"Another day in the exciting life of a school teacher," Elizabeth murmured to herself as she straightened the rows of desks.

Elizabeth found comfort in the rituals of her third-grade classroom. The recitation of times tables, the shuffling of workbooks, the rhythmic scratch of pencils. In this room, she felt in control. Children looked to her for guidance, hanging on her every word. Most days she could lose herself in the role of their teacher, mentor, or champion. But inevitably her composed mask would slip.

She might glance outside and catch a distant train whistle, reminding her of the wider world passing by. Other times, a precocious student would unwittingly stir a long-buried memory. Once little Amy Collins recited a poem that Elizabeth remembered Samuel reading aloud curled up on a picnic blanket, trading kisses with him between verses.

Samuel's family had lost everything when the Great Depression hit. Without even an in-person goodbye, they moved out of the village overnight in search of work. And like that, Elizabeth's first love was gone, leaving her heart not just bruised, but cracked fundamentally.

Now, when Elizabeth passed the boarded-up Lewis's house on her walks, she quickened her pace and averted her eyes. "Keep your eyes forward, Lizzy," she whispered. At night, though, in the silence of her room, letting her hair down and sinking into bed, Samuel still crept into her thoughts. That familiar straight tooth smile, dreamy brown eyes, and brown wavy hair. He had a scar on his forehead from falling out of a tree and she remembered the timbre of his voice singing folk songs. He was slender and stood around 5 foot 10 inches, which was not too tall or short, just right for her.

He was the type of guy who sat back in the class with his head buried in a book. He was never a show-off and just loved to write poetry and ride his bicycle. Elizabeth could still feel his comforting warm arms embracing her at night before she went into her house. The details were preserved perfectly in memory's amber.

The faint clang of the school bell stirred Elizabeth from her reverie. The Worthington School was still fairly new after being built in 1938. It contained six elementary classes and four junior high classrooms. Above the central entryway hung the original bell that one of the village founders, James Kilbourne, had originally purchased for the 1808 Worthington Academy Building. Little footsteps echoed down the hall as students began shuffling in. Elizabeth tidied her hair and straightened her dress, resuming the role she was here to play.

"Good morning class!" Elizabeth chirped brightly. "Let's all take our seats and get ready for a wonderful day of learning."

As the day progressed, Elizabeth fell into the comforting rhythm - reading aloud to the children, followed by reading circles, drilling arithmetic tables, and demonstrating proper penmanship techniques. She sometimes feared her days melted together into one long unending stretch, like gum pulled endlessly to see how far it would go before finally breaking. But she carried on, filling each moment with purposeful activity.

When the final bell rang, Elizabeth lingered to tidy up as tiny bodies dashed outside with carefree laughter. The room now empty, she clapped erasers vigorously, releasing dusty clouds into the afternoon light.

Finally, locking the door at 3:30, Elizabeth set off through the Village Green, the route that took her south on High Street past shops and offices buzzing with activity. Businessmen tipped their hats to ladies clutching parcels and purses. An elderly street sweeper bid her good afternoon. Elizabeth offered tight smiles in return. She envied their sense of forward motion. While others seemed propelled by purpose, she simply floated in placid waters, waiting to be directed downstream.

Making it back to New England Avenue and unlocking the heavy front door, Elizabeth entered the still house she had occupied alone for nearly a year now. She methodically hung her coat, placed her handbag on the small entry table, and smoothed the wrinkles from her dress. Glancing at the mirror, she fussed with a few stray hairs, tucking them back into her neat chignon. For a fleeting moment, she let her expression relax into naked vulnerability. But just as quickly the mask returned – everything tidy, ordered, proper.

Elizabeth moved through the silent rooms. Visions of her Irish mother fussing with perfectly arranged throw pillows and fretting over dusty furniture danced through her mind. Keeping up the house had become Elizabeth's way of holding things in place as if she could single-handedly stop things from aging through sheer willpower and some dusting. The repetitive cycle of cleaning, teaching, and checking on the store felt like she was living a life of her father's Motorola phonograph spinning a record on repeat.

"I wish there was some excitement around here," Elizabeth whispered to herself.

She entered the kitchen and began preparing a humble dinner for one. The Bird's Eye roast chicken had been defrosting all day in the refrigerator. She had learned to plan meals carefully to avoid waste. Elizabeth chopped carrots and parsley with meticulous precision, never leaving any food to waste. She added them to the pan. Sliding the chicken into the oven, she set the timer and tidied up as it cooked.

Sitting down at the table, the emptiness of the house closed in around her. Elizabeth missed her father's off-key humming while he ate. His amiable presence had once brought the rooms to life. Now the rooms were filled only with echoes of a home that used to be.

"Oh, Dad, I wish you were still here," Elizabeth sighed into the silence.

After eating, Elizabeth washed the dishes and set them on the drying rack, exactly parallel. Straightening table mats, aligning spice jars, inspecting for smudges on window panes – she tidied with diligence, as though aware things would unravel if she dared relax her grip.

When finished, Elizabeth settled into her father's worn armchair. She could still faintly smell the tobacco that used to cling to his cardigan. This chair, with its threadbare arms and sagging cushions, made her feel close to him again.

Her father had run the general store in the village faithfully for over 20 years. It was a modest but respectable business that supported their small family. After arriving from Sicily and spending time in New York City, he moved to Worthington where he worked his way up at the Red and White store. Eventually, he bought the business. Elizabeth fondly remembered scribbling her spelling words on the back of discarded receipt papers as she sat behind the counter after school. Her father would grin and sneak her pieces of peppermint candy when her mother wasn't looking. He would call her his little sicula, or Sicilian black bee, when she wore her yellow and black dress.

But as the Depression wore on, business at the store slowed to a trickle. Her father extended lines of credit to loyal customers hit hard by the economy. Some made good on their debts when they could, and others who couldn't pay left the village never to return. Each unpaid bill weighed on him more heavily. At that time, the store barely turned a profit, but he couldn't bear to shut its doors for good.

The day of the car accident, he suddenly was gone. He never got to truly enjoy the fruits of his labor and she never got to say goodbye to him. After he passed, Elizabeth was determined to keep the store open in his honor. Her mother protested that it made no sense for a young woman with a teaching career to take on such a burden. But it was the last real connection Elizabeth had to her father.

In her bedroom, Elizabeth gazed at the engagement photo occupying a prominent spot atop her dresser. It had been taken at an awkward dinner arranged by her mother. Elizabeth and her fiancé George sat stiffly side by side, barely touching—just two acquaintances who happened to be betrothed.

George, the accountant who had been checking the books for the Red and White store, had been begrudgingly hired by her father after he had an audit with the IRS. Elizabeth had suggested George to her father since she knew him in high school. After his death, George took over managing her father's accounts. George was meticulous and was also a bit boring. His only exciting side was his new Indian brand motorcycle. Her mother had suggested that she go on a date with him. After high school and with Samuel gone, she focused on her education rather than dating. But Elizabeth knew she wasn't getting any younger, so when he asked her out, she reluctantly agreed to go on the date. The date turned into multiple dates where he checked the store books and then took her out. It just became a routine.

Then finally it happened, the day George proposed to Elizabeth. It happened during a stilted conversation over an overcooked pot roast dinner at her home. The ring was presented like a business agreement. Never a romantic word passed his lips. But he came from a respectable family and promised stability - no small thing for a woman alone during such uncertain times. But she had known him since elementary school and he could provide her with a comfortable life. Elizabeth accepted his proposal, thinking she should be practical. Her mother beamed with delight.

Donning her nightgown, Elizabeth slid between cool sheets, but sleep evaded her for hours. Outside, the wind picked up into a dissonant howl. She tossed and turned, drifting in and out of sleep as a heavy fall rain began lashing at the windows and roof.

That night she dreamed of Samuel, his brown eyes dancing. They were young again, back by the Wilson Apple Orchard, just north of the village – their secret summer refuge, a little piece of paradise far from prying eyes. The years fell away as they swam in the cool water of the Olentangy River. Samuel's hands traced her arms, igniting a smoldering need. Thunder rumbled outside, jolting Elizabeth awake breathless and wanting.

In the darkness of her room, she could almost feel his lips on her neck, his fingers trailing her thigh. But reaching across the empty sheets found only cold, tangled linen. Elizabeth curled up tightly, clutching her pillow as longing gave way to sorrow.

"Oh, Samuel..." she whispered, a single tear rolling down her cheek. "I miss you still."

The next morning, Elizabeth arrived early at school. Paperwork cluttered her desk – both school preparations and store orders to fill, inventory to tally, and a pile of bills.

Elizabeth sighed and pushed the store paperwork aside and focused on her students. She found comfort in the classroom routines - reading aloud as children followed in their textbooks, drilling arithmetic tables in chorus, and trying to copy her perfect cursive script on their papers.

After the children dashed outside for recess, Elizabeth gazed absently out the window. She envied their youthful energy. The future stretched before them, unwritten. Watching a pair of birds dancing across the sky, she wondered what it would feel like to be so unencumbered and free.

After school, Elizabeth stopped by the Red and White on her way home. Stepping inside, she could almost imagine her father behind the counter, grinning as he filled tobacco tins for regular customers. There she greeted John, who still had pep after a day of managing.

"Good afternoon, John."

"Good afternoon, Elizabeth, how was school today?"

"Great, the children are working on their times tables. Did we get those new chocolates in stock?"

"Yes, sure did. They are called M and M's," John said.

He handed her a spoonful of the candy.

Elizabeth placed them in her mouth and started chewing.

"Oh, I better not bring these to class. The children will never stop asking for them!" Elizabeth said, smiling.

She then rolled up her sleeves and set to work. She began organizing shelves, sweeping the worn wooden floors, and dusting window sills. It was calming to keep busy, as if through sheer effort she could hold at bay the creeping decay she saw lurking in the cracks on the wooden floor.

After closing up, Elizabeth waved to John goodnight and walked parallel to High Street. As she started, Elizabeth heard a sudden loud noise.

She then heard a yell, "Get out of the way!"

She leaped out of the way while the woosh sound of an old Model T car plowed over the curb and hit the lamp pole.

With the smoke rising, the driver wiped his jacket and said, "I don't know what just happened, I lost control of the brakes!"

A burst of white light appeared with the sound of a flash bulb. It was Danny, a Worthington high school senior and aspiring photojournalist taking a photo.

"You could have been killed Miss Russo!" Danny exclaimed.

"Thank God, I'm alright Danny! Just in quite a shock. Fortunately, it doesn't appear the driver is hurt," Elizabeth said as she brushed her hands on her forehead.

"Elizabeth, are you okay?" yelled John running towards her.

"Yes, John, I'll be fine," her heart was beating quickly while she dusted off her dress.

"Ok, then go home and get a good night's sleep," replied John.

As Elizabeth walked home, she ran the scene of the accident over in her head. The yelling, the sound of the car crashing, and the whoosh of excitement as she jumped out of the way. She knew she was lucky and survived something that could have been horrible. Perhaps her father's spirit was looking over her shoulders. For that one fleeting moment, the cracks below the surface were smoothed by hope.

Chapter 2: An Unexpected Encounter

The shriek pierced the air of the schoolyard, startling Elizabeth from her distracted thoughts. Little Amy Collins lay sobbing on the ground, her knee bloodied from falling off the swing set. Elizabeth rushed over and scooped the child into her arms.

"Shh shh, you're alright my dear," she soothed, carrying Amy inside to clean and bandage the scrape. The girl winced as Elizabeth gently rubbed the wound with antiseptic.

"It stings, Miss Russo!" said Amy.

"I know it stings, but we've got to keep it clean. You're very brave," Elizabeth said as she finished wrapping the bandage. She gave Amy a reassuring hug, but inside, Elizabeth felt shaken. She blamed herself for not paying closer attention during recess. Her mind had been distracted. It kept wandering back to Samuel, conjuring up memories of her first love now lost. She went inside to inform Principal Gentry of Amy's accident.

"Principal Gentry, I must inform you that Amy Collins took a fall from the swing set today during recess. I cleaned and wrapped up the cut. She's ok now." said Elizabeth.

"Oh, dear. Well, I better reach out to Mrs. Collins. Thank you, Elizabeth, for letting me know. I appreciate your hard work." he replied.

Elizabeth nodded and walked back to her classroom.

The final school bell rang at last. Elizabeth tidied up the classroom from the day's lessons.

She turned to see Mrs. Collins storming in, face like a thundercloud.

"Mrs. Collins! What a surprise. How is Amy feeling?" Elizabeth asked gently.

"She is in dreadful pain, no thanks to you!" Mrs. Collins said sharply. "What kind of teacher lets a child get so injured on her watch?"

Elizabeth felt her cheeks flush. "I'm sorry about the accident, it all happened so fast—"

"Sorry, doesn't help my poor Amy!" Mrs. Collins interrupted. "She could have broken her leg out there while you daydreamed. I've got a mind to speak to the school board about your negligence."

"Now Mrs. Collins," Elizabeth replied firmly, "accidents sometimes happen on the playground. That's part of childhood. Amy is a resilient girl, and I'm sure she'll heal quickly."

"Hmph! Well, she certainly won't be healing under your careless supervision," Mrs. Collins huffed. "I expect the board will see a reason to find a more suitable teacher."

She turned and marched out, leaving Elizabeth stunned and shaken in the empty classroom.

Elizabeth's head was spinning.

"Yesterday the car accident and now this incident?" Elizabeth said to herself.

"It wasn't your fault Elizabeth," came a voice from the hallway. "That could have happened to any of us."

It was Debbie Greener, the fourth-grade teacher across the hallway.

"Elizabeth, accidents do happen, and Amy's fine. Don't let Mrs. Collins get the best of you! We've all had a run-in with her at one time or another."

"Thank you, Debbie, you know you are an inspiration not only to your class but to me as well."

Elizabeth felt a little better. Miss Greener walked out of the room and Elizabeth packed her tote bag and headed back home.

She turned west down Granville Road, crossing High Street. She wasn't in the mood to see George at the Red and White Store, so she kept walking onto Oxford Street. She walked a block past the tidy houses. Then, she turned right onto New England Avenue to her house. Up ahead, a familiar figure stood stiffly next to his motorcycle in her driveway. George. She stifled a sigh.

"Hello George," Elizabeth greeted politely.

"Elizabeth, we must discuss wedding plans. I was thinking that June would allow ample time for preparations."

She hesitated. "George, it's been rather a long day. Amy Collins took a tumble at recess and it gave me a scare."

George's brow furrowed. "Children fall, it's to be expected. But we cannot delay wedding planning. The church will be booked up," he insisted. His forcefulness was grating after the stresses of the day.

They stood in terse silence for a moment. Then George straightened, adjusting his tie. "Fine, we'll discuss this later. I should be getting home. Goodbye, Elizabeth."

As George pulled out of the driveway, Elizabeth heard a sound. It was Betty Whimsfeld, her eccentric neighbor, tidying the front porch.

"Good afternoon, Elizabeth! Cracker Jack of a day!"

Elizabeth turned to see Betty waving from across the porch.

Betty smiled as she walked over holding a broom and wearing a fake pearl necklace. She was around her mother's age, in her sixties. Even though she lived next door to Elizabeth's family, Elizabeth never really got to know her.

"Betty, you're too kind. Let me help with that," Elizabeth offered, reaching for the broom.

Betty smiled warmly with her curly salt and pepper hair blowing in the gentle breeze.

"Oh, nonsense dear, you've had a long day! The leaves are already coming down! Let me help sweep your porch. It gets me outdoors enjoying the fresh fall air."

"Well, I appreciate your offer Betty, but I can manage," replied Elizabeth.

"Of course! Now, how are those wedding plans coming along?" Betty asked with her eyes bulging from the thick lenses of her glasses. "George seems very eager to tie the knot."

Elizabeth shifted, busying herself with straightening her tote bag. "Oh, we're still finalizing details. You know how it is, so many decisions to make."

Betty nodded knowingly.

"That George seems a very proper and respectable young man," Betty said, giving Elizabeth a knowing look. "But I must say, he doesn't seem to have much spark or spontaneity, does he?

Not like that charming Samuel you used to spend time with when you were younger. Oh, you two were lovely together! He could always make you laugh and bring such joy to your face. And those poems he wrote were simply mesmerizing!

This George, well, he may be a nice guy, but he doesn't quite have that special something. It's not like that magic you and Samuel shared. Now I'm just a sentimental old woman, but I think when it comes to marriage you should marry your best friend, someone who makes you glow inside and out!"

"Betty, it's been five years since Samuel left me," said Elizabeth with her head down.

Betty smiled warmly and patted Elizabeth's hand. "Just an old romantic's ramblings, my dear."

"Indeed, indeed. By the way, I'm still trying to find my Jell-O recipe. I must make it for you. It's delectable!

"I appreciate that, Betty. Have a lovely evening!" Elizabeth waived as her kind neighbor headed home.

She appreciated her neighbor's efforts to brighten her mood. However, the reference to the wedding had only added to the unease simmering inside her.

Alone again, Elizabeth felt the emptiness of the house acutely. She missed her mother, Anna. She had been in Cincinnati for months now looking after Elizabeth's Aunt Gracie, who'd fallen ill.

After washing up from dinner, Elizabeth found herself restless. It was getting cooler out but she felt she needed to get out of the house. Elizabeth slipped a light jacket over her dress for an evening stroll. Just then the phone rang. Elizabeth picked up the receiver.

"Hello, is this Miss Russo?"

"Yes."

"This is an operator with the American Telephone and Telegraph Company. You have a long-distance phone call from Cincinnati from Anna Russo. Will you accept it?" The operator asked.

"Yes," responded Elizabeth.

There was a slight pause with a faint voice in the background.

"Hello, Elizabeth?" a female said on the phone line.

"Mother?" Elizabeth replied.

"Yes, dear, I have sad news for you. Your Aunt Gracie has gotten worse and has to go to the hospital. I don't know if she will make it through to next week. I was wondering if you could take the 9 AM Greyhound down to Price Hill, just outside of Cincinnati, to visit us?"

"Of course, Mom, I can make it down first thing tomorrow morning."

"Wonderful sweetheart! We will see you around 11:30 Saturday morning at the bus station. Have a good night."

"Goodnight, Mom, my thoughts are with Aunt Gracie and Uncle Herb. Bye-bye." Elizabeth responded as she hung up the phone.

ELIZABETH WAS IN A bit of a shock. First, the stress from Amy falling, and now Aunt Gracie. She recently received a letter from her mother that stated Aunt Gracie had taken a turn for the better. Well, that turn must have had an added twist on the road.

The sun was just starting to set and Elizabeth knew she couldn't sit in the house alone. She had to get out. She needed a change and wanted to feel free. She slipped into her blue dress and walked up to Oxford Street towards the Village Green. She crossed High Street and wandered past the Worthington Savings Bank. Next to it was the little white building where Samuel's uncle operated an insurance store. The water tower was looming behind it and there was Ault Hardware. She admired the storefronts, imagining herself a carefree shopper without a worry.

Next to the hardware was her father's grocery, The Red and White. It had a Wonder Bread sign out front along with a "Have a Coke" sign. Elizabeth wanted a Coke but she was craving something a little bit stronger. The store was closed for the evening but there was John inside. If it weren't for John and a few other local boys, she wouldn't know how she would manage the grocery and keep her teaching job, especially with her mother in Cincinnati. She was one of the lucky ones, who had a job. Others weren't as lucky.

The door opened, "Come on in Elizabeth," said John. "I'm just wrapping up. How was your day?"

"My Aunt Gracie has taken a turn for the worse. I'm going to have to take the bus tomorrow down to Cincinnati."

"I'm sorry to hear that, Elizabeth. I know she has been sick for a while now."

"Thanks, John,"

As Elizabeth peered at the cash register, she looked down at the counter. She saw the shape of a little female dancing figure.

Elizabeth squinted for a moment, "Is that my ballerina music box?"

"Is this yours?" replied John. "I found it back in the stock room when I was moving some Wheat Krispies cereal boxes."

"My father gave this to me when I was a little girl. I haven't seen this in years." Elizabeth turned the latch and let the music box play. The little ballerina twirled as the music played. Elizabeth looked up at John and smiled.

"You know, John, when I was young, I wanted to be a ballerina. Unfortunately, life gets in the way. I don't know how you found this, but that just made my day!" Elizabeth felt as if her father had just given her a little wink and a nod.

"I'll let you finish up here up here, John. I know my father would be proud of the work you are doing at the store."

"I hope he would be. Good night, Elizabeth!"

"Good night," Elizabeth said as she shut the door and walked down the street towards the Sinclair Service Station. She looked across the street. Drawn by its warm glow, she approached the New England Inn.

She peered inside and saw a few familiar faces. She walked in and selected a small corner table to sit by herself. Elizabeth typically wouldn't enter a place like this alone but this was where a lot of residents socialized. When she sat down, she thought of the Coke sign out in front of the Red and White store and knew what she would order.

"Good evening, Miss Russo. You look lovely in that blue dress. That color is calm and confident. Are you feeling calm and confident?" grinned Jimmy the bartender.

"Why yes, Jimmy. Matter of fact, I am feeling calm and confident," smiled Elizabeth.

"Wonderful! What will it be tonight?" asked the bartender as he walked up to the table.

"Jimmy, I'll take a whiskey and Coke."

"Whiskey and Coke? Do you want those out in two separate glasses?" asked Jimmy.

"No sir, I'll have them poured together. I'm feeling uncharacteristically daring tonight," replied Elizabeth.

"Whatever you say, Miss Russo. It's just that I've never heard of such a thing," said Jimmy.

"You'll just have to try one for yourself," Elizabeth said with a wink.

"Well, that sounds better than tequila and Coke!" smiled Jimmy.

There were some of the regulars sitting at the bar. Mr. Deckard, owner of her father's competing store, the Home Market; Mr. Price, an employee at Potter Lumber; Dr. Bentley, the town's physician smoking a cigar, and Jane, Elizabeth's hairdresser. They were all talking and laughing, probably about the same old things. Sometimes it feels that nothing changes in Worthington.

A tune was playing on the radio. It was an old song, but one that you could whistle to. "When the flowers grow, as the summer goes, I want to hold your hand. When the leaves fall, bring love to all, I want to hold your hand". Jimmy brought her the drink and Elizabeth took a sip. It warmed her like a hypnotic glass of sweet warm milk. She started to drift to the melody of the tune.

As Elizabeth sipped, her eyes began wandering over the lively place. Just then, the door swung open letting in a cool draft. Everyone turned around to look. There, stumbling in was Hobo Jeff. An old veteran of the Great War who had stumbled on hard times. He looked over to Elizabeth and said, "Mind giving me a sip of whiskey, Love, to warm this old man's heart?"

"Jeff," Jimmy cut in, "I told you that you cannot just walk in here and ask our guests for drinks. Be off with you!"

Hobo Jeff turned around, looked at the bartender, and said, "Well, it looks like it hasn't warmed up around here!" as he stumbled back outside. Jimmy shook his head as Elizabeth smiled. "Some things never change." She murmured.

Elizabeth looked up and saw Jane get up from the bar and walk towards her. Elizabeth didn't want to be bothered tonight, especially by her. Jane knew all the community gossip working at the Lady Alice Beauty Salon across the street. With the spill that little Amy Collins had today, Elizabeth knew word would move fast.

"Elizabeth! How are you, my dear? I heard Mrs. Collins say that Amy fell at school today. Is she alright?" asked Jane.

Elizabeth was getting ready to respond when something caught her eye in the back room just past the bar.

Her breath caught. This was no fleeting glimpse or trick of the mind. It was Samuel!

Her eyes locked on him across the crowded room. Samuel's companions seemed to fade into the background as she gazed at him with an intensity that made her shiver before she could even barely process what was happening.

"Elizabeth," Jane asked again, "Is Amy alright?"

Elizabeth's heart hammered in her chest. She opened her mouth to speak, but no words came out. Just then, a loud burst of laughter from the bar broke the spell. Samuel glanced over his shoulder uneasily.

Did he see her? He had grown and was in a dapper brown suit.

Elizabeth, who quickly took one large sip of the drink, could only nod. With a sad smile, Samuel dipped his head politely and turned around to his party. Elizabeth clutched her drink knowing they hadn't spoken for five years. What did it all mean?

"Elizabeth!" Jane almost shouted, "You're pale. My goodness, are you alright?"

"I've just seen a ghost from the past." Elizabeth hurriedly replied. "I need to leave at once!"

Elizabeth took one large last sip of her drink and placed the glass down on the table. She made a run for the door.

"Miss Russo, ahem." beckoned Jimmy with his hand raised out.

"Oh, sorry Jimmy," said Elizabeth as she placed a dime in his hand and began to rush off.

"And don't forget you have a hair appointment with me on Monday," Jane said with an inquisitive grin.

Elizabeth hurriedly opened the door and stepped out onto the sidewalk. Her mind swirled with more questions than ever. It felt like a fog had rolled into her mind. Elizabeth wavered between excitement, imagining scenarios where she and Samuel reconciled, and despair knowing she had pledged herself to another man. She knew it was him. She couldn't mistake those twinkling brown eyes. She needed to get home, though. She had a big day ahead of her tomorrow.

Chapter 3: Journey to the Queen City

Elizabeth awoke before dawn, heart pounding. Today was the day she would go to Cincinnati to see her ailing Aunt Gracie. But also heavy on her mind was Samuel, who had appeared at the New England Inn the night before.

Shaking off dreams filled with his memory, Elizabeth washed and dressed efficiently in her traveling clothes. She made herself a quick breakfast, but could barely eat from the nervous flutters in her stomach.

Outside, the late September air was unusually crisp and cool. Elizabeth pulled her coat tighter as she walked briskly with the suitcase in hand to the Greyhound stop. A gust of cold air blew at the stop in front of Birnie's Drug Store, across the street from her father's store. Some lamps were glowing warmly in a few shop windows and Milkman Bailey was making his rounds.

Elizabeth arrived on time as the bus pulled up with a squeal of brakes. She presented her ticket with cold, trembling fingers and found her seat. Glancing at her watch, she saw it was precisely 9 AM.

With a roar of its engines, the bus lurched forward and they were off. Elizabeth gazed out the window as familiar sights rolled by on High Street - the steepled church, the grocer's and barber's shops. All were slowly waking to meet the new day.

Soon they were on the outskirts of downtown, picking up speed as they joined the main highway heading south. Columbus appeared on the horizon as a cluster of buildings in the distance. But rather than its usual thrilling bustle, this morning the city seemed shrouded in the same somber quiet as Elizabeth's hometown.

As the bus rumbled on, Elizabeth tried to focus on the book in her hands. But the words blurred together meaninglessly. Her mind kept drifting back to her high school days with Samuel. She saw his smile and heard his laugh. Felt the brush of his hand against hers as they walked together.

Back then, weekends often found them escaping town on bicycle adventures. Samuel would arrive early, knocking at her door with a secretive grin. They'd pedal briskly out Willow Brook Road, the wind whipping their hair.

Just through the old Wilson apple orchard was their favorite spot, a secluded bend along the Olentangy River. Samuel would spread out the picnic lunch he had packed while Elizabeth admired the glint of sunlight on the river.

After eating, they would lounge on the grass together while he read poetry that he wrote. The one that always made her giggle was one called, "My Sicilian Sassafras". Samuel would read it to her,

"A playful ode to my darling Elizabeth,
Whose smiles lift my spirits like the sun breaking dawn.
Eyes shining bright as stars over Worthington,
With laughter warm as apple pie fresh from the oven.
My heart stirs like leaves rustling in autumn's wind
When you pass by, your lovely dark hair curled just so.
No mystery or darkness can extinguish the light
Of your intrepid heart, you wonderful darling.
Let us stroll Worthington's lanes hand in hand.
While cardinals sing songs of our renewed love.
No more rhyme or reason when we're apart -
My heart belongs to you, my sweet Sicilian sassafras."

All too soon, the afternoon would fade, and they'd bicycle back before dark with flushed cheeks and racing hearts.

A bump jolted Elizabeth from her reverie. She looked around in surprise to see they had stopped in a small town. Washington Courthouse read the sign at the bus stop where some passengers were disembarking.

The bus driver announced a 30-minute break. Elizabeth walked out of the bus and joined the queue entering the nearby diner, too distracted to be hungry but knowing she should eat. The short respite gave her time to regain composure before the final leg to Cincinnati.

The bus depot diner was nearly empty at this hour. Elizabeth ordered a coffee to be polite, though her nervous stomach rebelled at the thought of food. She sipped the hot bitter liquid slowly, watching the hands on the clock tick by.

Back on the bus, the caffeine coursed through her veins, making her restless. As the bus once again lurched into motion and raced an endless flat landscape of farms and fields, Elizabeth's thoughts also raced.

Where had Samuel been all these years? What had his life become after they parted ways? Had he married, or had children? She knew nothing of what he did during the long lean years of the Depression. And now suddenly he was back in town. Why? She had to talk to him, to understand what it meant. Elizabeth gazed out at the fields rolling by, steeling herself for the conversation ahead.

The coffee stirred a tempest of excitement and anxiety within her. Elizabeth's emotions swung wildly between anticipation of seeing Samuel again and doubt over the wisdom of reopening old wounds.

Her mind then turned to George, her dutiful fiancé awaiting her return. He offered security, stability, and all that she needed to settle down properly. But when she pictured him, Elizabeth felt no quickening of her pulse, no bubbling joy. Not like with Samuel, but that was six years ago.

"Get your head together Lizzy!" Elizabeth said to herself.

Outside the bus windows, the scenery blurred past unnoticed. Elizabeth shifted in her seat, wiping the dew on the window, unable to get comfortable.

She had to talk to Samuel and look into those warm brown eyes again. She needed to understand what his return meant. Until she did, Elizabeth knew her memories would continue tormenting her heart and taunting her future happiness.

As the bus droned on, Elizabeth slipped into a dreamlike state, tossing between fitful bouts of sleeping and waking. Her thoughts rolled like the passing countryside, up and down through memories and possibilities.

One moment she pictured herself gliding down the aisle toward steadfast George, ready to begin a sensible new life. But then her dreams would transform into bike rides with playful Samuel, filled with laughter and stolen kisses that tasted so sweet.

Back and forth her imagination swung between the two men. When dreaming of Samuel, joy illuminated her soul. But those carefree days were long gone. The Samuel she knew had disappeared without a word.

Anger suddenly pierced through Elizabeth's reverie. After all they had shared, he had not bothered to write even once during their years apart. She had waited in vain for some sign while trying to mend her broken heart.

Elizabeth knew Samuel had left to work his grandparents' farm in Kansas when the Depression struck. All he did was leave her one small card in her mailbox stating that he was leaving. But in her mind, that did not excuse his silence. He could have reached out, and let her know he still cared. The gulf of unanswered questions between them still ached.

The bus hit a bump and Elizabeth jolted awake, cheeks wet with tears. Disoriented, she looked around to see city buildings gliding past the window. They were in Cincinnati.

"You have arrived at your destination, the Queen City!" the driver announced cheerfully. Elizabeth hastily dried her eyes, trying to compose herself before the bus rolled to a stop.

Stepping off the bus into the morning sunlight, Elizabeth immediately spotted her mother and Uncle Herbert waiting beside his polished blue Studebaker Champion.

"Lizzie, you're here!" her mother cried, rushing over to embrace her. Elizabeth sank into the comforting familiarity of her mother's arms.

"Well, hey there Lizzie girl, you're looking as pretty as a new penny," her uncle said with a wink, giving her shoulder an affectionate squeeze. Even with worry weighing on him, her uncle's humor shone through.

The three climbed into the car and were soon gliding through the streets. To Elizabeth, the bustling city felt thrillingly alive, like New York itself.

"How was your journey, dear?" her mother asked.

"Uneventful, thankfully," Elizabeth said. "And how is Aunt Gracie holding up?"

Her uncle shook his head grimly. "Not well I'm afraid. She's fading faster than the leaves in autumn."

"Now Herbert, you mustn't talk about your wife like that," her mother chided. She turned to Elizabeth with a brave smile. "Gracie is comfortable and holding her own for now."

Elizabeth nodded, bracing herself for what was to come. She reached over and gave her mother's hand a comforting squeeze. Aunt Gracie was 10 years older than her mother and, Elizabeth thought, wiser.

They soon pulled up at the imposing hospital building. Inside, the smell of antiseptic hung heavy in the air. Elizabeth shivered as they stepped into the rickety elevator cage that took them up to the third floor.

Down the long corridor was Aunt Gracie's room. Elizabeth hesitated at the door, pulse racing. She felt her mother's hand on her back, guiding her forward.

Elizabeth opened the door and walked inside the room.

Aunt Gracie looked so small and frail in the hospital bed, but her face lit up when she saw Elizabeth.

"There's my beautiful girl," she said in a tired voice. "Come give your auntie a kiss."

"Oh Elizabeth, it's so wonderful to see your sweet face," Aunt Gracie said weakly but with a bright smile. "Come sit by me dear."

Elizabeth pulled a chair close to the bedside and gently grasped her aunt's frail hand.

"Do you remember when we used to bake sugar cookies together in the kitchen?" Aunt Gracie asked. "Even when sugar was scarce, we'd always manage to whip up a batch."

Elizabeth nodded, choking back tears at the fond memory.

Aunt Gracie peered closely at her. "But you seem sad, dear. What is it? You mustn't fret about me."

"It's nothing, just worried for you," Elizabeth said, avoiding her aunt's searching look.

But Aunt Gracie patted her hand knowingly. "Come now, tell me what's really bothering you."

Elizabeth hesitated, then confessed in a rush, "I saw Samuel in town last night. For the first time in five years."

Aunt Gracie's face lit up. "Samuel! Oh, I remember how you two used to be inseparable. Young love such an exciting time."

Blushing, Elizabeth admitted "Seeing him again stirred up old feelings I thought were long gone. Feelings I haven't had in so long..." she trailed off uncertainly.

Aunt Gracie beckoned Elizabeth closer with a tired but radiant smile. "Come here, dear, I have something for you."

When Elizabeth leaned in, Aunt Gracie unclasped her pearl necklace and pressed it into Elizabeth's hand. "This is yours now. It will bring you clarity. Follow where your heart leads you."

Overcome with emotion, all Elizabeth could do was nod gratefully as her aunt settled back onto her pillow and drifted off to sleep.

Exiting Aunt Gracie's room, Elizabeth found her mother and Uncle Herbert waiting in the hallway. Seeing her daughter's tear-stained face, Elizabeth's mother rushed over.

"Oh dear, what is it? Is Gracie alright?" she asked worriedly.

Unable to speak, Elizabeth simply held out the necklace. Her mother's eyes widened in recognition.

"Gracie gave this to you?" she said in a hushed voice. Elizabeth nodded, fresh tears falling.

Uncle Herbert stepped forward and put a comforting hand on each of their shoulders. "Now, now, no more tears today. Gracie wouldn't want that." He gave them a gentle smile.

"Ladies, I know just the thing to lift your spirits. What do you say to a day on the town, just the two of you?"

Elizabeth and her mother looked uncertain, but Uncle Herbert was already pulling out his wallet. He pressed a crisp $50 bill into his sister-in-law's hand.

"Herbert, really we couldn't..." she protested, but he held up a hand.

"Now Anna, it's been too long since you've had a proper ladies' day out. It's what Gracie would want. I'm just sorry I can't tag along myself," he said with a wink.

"Now take this and go get yourselves something nice at Mabley and Carew's. Then, a bite to eat at the Netherland Plaza. Uncle's orders!"

Seeing the twinkle in his eye, Elizabeth felt her spirit lift just a little. She embraced her uncle gratefully, then hooked her arm through her mother's. The two women made their way out into the sunny autumn day, sharing memories of Gracie all the way.

At the hospital curb, they managed to hail a cab.

"Where to, ladies?" the cabbie asked cheerfully.

"Mabley and Carew's department store, please," Elizabeth's mother replied as they climbed inside.

Soon they pulled up at the iconic department store. Inside, the two women browsed the latest fashions, marveling at the variety throughout the afternoon.

Elizabeth selected a few dresses to try on, looking for just the right one. Finally, she emerged in an elegant emerald green chiffon dress with matching kitten heels. The color perfectly complemented Aunt Gracie's necklace.

"Oh Elizabeth, it's perfect!" her mother declared. "And it brings out your beautiful eyes."

Buoyed by the success, Elizabeth's mother also found a lovely new dress, a flowing chiffon number in her favorite shade of violet.

After completing their purchases, the pair emerged from the store in high spirits. Elizabeth tucked her arm through her mother's as they strolled down the street toward the Netherland Plaza Hotel.

Entering the grand lobby, Elizabeth and her mother knew they couldn't dine in their traveling clothes.

"Let's pop into the ladies' room to change," Elizabeth's mother suggested.

In the marble restroom, the two women squeezed into a stall together. They helped each other out of their old dresses and into the new finery, giggling like schoolgirls in their cramped quarters.

Elizabeth's mother stuffed their discarded clothes into her bag, while Elizabeth freshened up in the mirror. She carefully fastened Aunt Gracie's necklace around her neck and added a touch of lipstick and mascara.

"Just one more thing," her mother said, pulling a flower out of her bag and pinning it on Elizabeth's new dress. "There, perfect!"

Stepping out of the restroom, Elizabeth and her mother were dazzled by the splendor of the Netherland Plaza. The lobby was a masterpiece of French Art Deco design, with rare Brazilian rosewood paneling and elaborate brass metalwork.

As they glided arm in arm towards the restaurant, their high heels clicked rhythmically on the shiny marble floors. Above them rose a vaulted ceiling decorated with ornate plaster moldings. Crystal chandeliers cast a warm glow over the space.

They passed through the legendary Hall of Mirrors, feeling as glamorous as movie stars. The mirrored walls reflected their images infinitely down the grand corridor lined with planters of palm trees. It was like walking through the Palace of Versailles itself.

Everywhere they looked, Elizabeth and her mother saw exquisite details - hand-painted murals, inlaid wood floors, gilded accents on columns and railings. Cincinnati's crowning architectural jewel enveloped them in luxury.

As the maître d' led Elizabeth and her mother into the elegant restaurant, they were swallowed in a symphony of sights and sounds.

The murmur of intimate conversations and the gentle clink of silverware on fancy plates filled the air. Occasionally, a burst of laughter would ring out from a table before hushing again. Waiters in crisp white jackets floated between tables, their footfalls muffled by thick carpets.

Delicious aromas wafted from the bustling kitchen, making Elizabeth's empty stomach rumble. The rich scent of smoking steaks mingled with the brightness of fresh lemon and herbs. Warm yeast rolls and the sweet tang of butter completed the mouthwatering medley.

A piano player in the corner accompanied the diners with gentle jazz tunes. The live music lent a convivial, celebratory air to the scene as friends dined together amidst the chandeliers' soft glow.

Overall, the sounds and smells combined to create an ambience of refinement and community. Elizabeth squeezed her mother's hand, communicating wordlessly her joy at sharing this exquisite experience.

The maître d' led Elizabeth and her mother to a cozy table near the piano. As they settled into the plush chairs, a well-dressed waiter approached with menus.

"Welcome, ladies. My name is Thomas and I'll be taking care of you today," he said with a charming smile. "May I start you off with something to drink?"

"I think some champagne is to celebrate this special occasion," Elizabeth's mother declared.

"What a wonderful idea," Elizabeth agreed.

Thomas nodded. "An excellent choice. I'll return promptly with a bottle of our finest."

After he stepped away, Elizabeth grasped her mother's hand across the table. "Thank you for this beautiful day, Mother. I know Aunt Gracie would have loved it."

"Of course, my dear. Gracie would be so pleased to see her necklace being worn and enjoyed."

Just then Thomas returned, expertly popping open the champagne bottle. "Are we ready to order?" he asked.

Elizabeth and her mother clinked their bubbling glasses together. "I believe we are," Elizabeth said.

As Elizabeth and her mother sipped their champagne, a striking woman in a red sequined dress stepped up to the small stage. The chatter quieted as she adjusted the microphone.

"Good evening, ladies and gentlemen," she purred in a silky voice. "My name is Vivian and I'll be providing this evening's entertainment."

She nodded to the pianist and began singing in a sultry, bluesy tone. Smooth as velvet, she effortlessly glided up and down the notes. Vivian closed her eyes, swaying gently to the melody, lost in the lyrics of love and heartbreak.

She had voluminous curls the color of mahogany that shone under the stage lights. Her skin seemed to glow against the shimmering crimson dress that hugged every curve.

Vivian's voice swelled with emotion on the slower ballads, vulnerability cracking through her sophisticated demeanor. During upbeat numbers, she would shimmy and snap her fingers playfully, flashing a dazzling smile.

Elizabeth was enthralled, transported by the power and intimacy of Vivian's performance. She imagined herself dancing in her new dress and necklace with Samuel dressed in the brown suit she saw at the Inn. For those moments, Vivian held the hearts of the entire room in her hands.

When the last haunting note faded, the audience erupted in enthusiastic applause. Vivian took a bow, blowing a kiss before gliding off stage, her stilettos clicking across the floor.

After applauding the stunning performance, Elizabeth and her mother turned their attention to the delicious meal set before them.

Elizabeth had chosen the herb-roasted chicken breast served atop a bed of wild rice pilaf. The tender chicken was juicy and flavorful, complemented nicely by the fluffy, buttery rice. Asparagus spears roasted with lemon and olive oil completed the plate.

Meanwhile, Elizabeth's mother savored the baked salmon filet with dill cream sauce. The fish flaked apart easily under her fork, moist and delicate. It was paired with roasted fingerling potatoes still warm from the oven and crisp enough to crunch.

For dessert, they decided to share the decadent chocolate mousse cake. Each silky bite dissolved on the tongue into a rich dark cocoa essence. They ate slowly, savoring each luscious morsel.

The champagne had left them feeling effervescent and a little giddy. Their laughter came frequently and easily, as they chatted away between blissful bites. The delicious food tasted even better when seasoned by their shared conversation and memories.

After finishing the last crumb of their cake, Elizabeth and her mother were surprised when their waiter, Thomas, appeared bearing two elegant dessert plates.

"The chef would like you to try his latest creations," he announced with a little bow.

On Elizabeth's plate was an airy vanilla soufflé served with a tangy raspberry compote. Her spoon cut easily through the puffed creamy top to reveal the still-molten center. The contrast of the light soufflé and tart fruit sauce was sheer bliss.

Her mother's plate held a beautifully layered matcha green tea Mille crepe cake. Each paper-thin crepe was brushed with a delicate matcha cream before being stacked tall. Dusting of powdered sugar added a final touch of sweetness while allowing the deep green tea flavor to shine.

As the women slowly savored the exquisite desserts, Elizabeth raised her champagne flute. "To Gracie - thank you for bringing us together today," she toasted.

"To Gracie," her mother echoed with happy tears in her eyes.

Elizabeth felt certain her dear aunt would be pleased to see them enjoying life's amazing pleasures together.

Chapter 4: Thunder Rumbles, Questions Loom

The autumn sun was lowering in the sky as Elizabeth and her mother exited the grand doors of the Netherland Plaza. Arm in arm, they strolled to the line of waiting taxis and hailed one to take them back to Price Hill.

As the cab pulled away from the curb, the driver asked, "Where to, ladies?"

"Oh, we're heading to Price Hill, please," Elizabeth's mother responded.

As they drove, Elizabeth gazed out the window deep in thought. They passed an Empress Chili shop, its neon sign just flickering on in the dusk. She wondered if Samuel had tried Cincinnati's famous chili and imagined bringing him here, seeing his face light up after the first mouthwatering bite.

Elizabeth scolded herself internally. She shouldn't be having such fanciful thoughts about Samuel. Not when she had pledged herself to George back home. But still, she couldn't help but imagine Samuel's reaction if he saw her in this elegant new dress, wearing Aunt Gracie's necklace. Surely, he would be mesmerized.

The cab began steadily climbing the steep streets that gave Price Hill its name. Elizabeth reminded herself that she and Samuel were long ago and far away now. She was an engaged woman. Still, seeing him again, if only for a moment, had reawakened dormant feelings and hopes inside her.

Up the hill, they continued as Elizabeth gazed out at the houses flickering past, as unsure about her future as the dusky sunset fading into nightfall around them.

The cab wound its way up the steep, curving streets. Elizabeth gripped the door handle as they swung around tight bends, the buildings and sidewalks tilting at gravity-defying angles.

It felt strangely reminiscent of her shifting perspectives and tilting emotions over the past day. First came the surprise encounter with Samuel, rattling the foundations of her heart. Then, joyful moments laughing with family before the sobering visit with ailing Aunt Gracie.

The soaring highs and plummeting lows had left Elizabeth feeling dizzy and unsettled. Like this cab careening around hazardous hills and valleys, life had thrown her on a rollercoaster ride when all she expected was a straightforward journey.

As the streets leveled out atop Price Hill, Elizabeth glanced at her mother. She took comfort in knowing that despite life's twists and turns, she could rely on the unwavering support of family. With their steadying presence, she could regain balance while navigating her way forward, wherever the road may lead next.

The cab rolled to a stop in front of Aunt Gracie and Uncle Herbert's cozy home. Elizabeth noticed right away that the front porch light was off, unusual on a cool autumn evening.

She and her mother made their way up the walk. Before they could even knock, the door swung open revealing a grim-faced Uncle Herbert. His eyes were red-rimmed and missing their habitual twinkle.

"Ladies, I'm afraid Gracie passed away this afternoon," he said heavily.

Elizabeth and her mother both gasped, fresh tears springing to their eyes, as they embraced Uncle Herbert.

"Oh, Herbert, I'm so sorry," Elizabeth's mother choked out. "How are you holding up?"

He shook his head sadly. "It's a terrible blow. But she went peacefully with me there. And I know it would have brought her great happiness to know you two were enjoying a beautiful day together."

"That's exactly what we were talking about at dinner," Elizabeth said. "All our favorite memories of Gracie. She was there with us in spirit."

Uncle Herbert managed a faint smile at that. "Good, I'm glad to hear it. Now come inside, I could use the company tonight."

The three crossed the threshold together, united in their grief but drawing strength from shared love and loss.

After sitting up late into the night reminiscing with Uncle Herbert, he finally said "Ladies, it's getting late. We should all try to get some rest."

Elizabeth hugged her uncle goodnight and retired to the guest bedroom. As she lay in bed, thoughts of Aunt Gracie flooded her mind memories of baking cookies, exchanging secrets, laughing until their sides ached. Silent tears fell remembering her dear aunt's vibrant spirit.

Eventually, Gracie faded from her mind, replaced by Samuel's face. Elizabeth thought back on all the times Samuel had comforted her through life's difficulties with his easy laugh and strong embrace.

In contrast, while steady and reliable, George had never been one for heartfelt words or gestures. She knew he would offer practical support if she confided her grief. But it wouldn't be the same as Samuel wrapping her in his arms, soothing her with whispers that everything would be okay.

Exhausted by the emotional day, Elizabeth finally drifted off to sleep. She dreamt she was walking hand in hand with Samuel down a sunlit road, weightless and unburdened.

Elizabeth was startled awake by a knock at her door. "Elizabeth, it's time to get up," came her mother's muffled voice. "We're going to church while your uncle makes arrangements at the funeral home."

Still bleary, Elizabeth blinked open her eyes and stared up at the ceiling. The grief of yesterday came flooding back. She slowly dressed in a simple navy blue dress, pinning on the hat she had bought with her mother.

When she emerged, Uncle Herbert was waiting by the front door looking weary but composed. "The cab will be here any minute to take you ladies to St. Francis Xavier," he informed them.

Turning to Elizabeth, he added "I likely won't see you again before your trip home. Travel safely and have a good week teaching."

"Are you sure I shouldn't stay and help?" Elizabeth asked.

But Uncle Herbert patted her hand. "Your mother will be here. Get back to your students."

He pulled an envelope from his pocket with a grin. "Here is your ticket home," he said, pressing it into her hand.

Elizabeth looked down in surprise. "A train ticket?"

"Yes, I wanted you to travel back in style," he said with a gentle smile. "Now, get going and give those kids an extra hug from Uncle Herbert."

Elizabeth embraced him tightly, not knowing when they would meet again. As the cab pulled up, she dabbed her eyes and followed her mother down the walk.

The taxi carried Elizabeth and her mother down the winding hills into downtown Cincinnati. As they drove, her mother pointed out landmarks to distract Elizabeth from her grief.

"There's St. Francis Xavier Church up ahead. Did you know it was dedicated back in 1826?" she commented. Elizabeth nodded, gazing up at the imposing Gothic revival structure standing tall above the neighborhood.

She appreciated her mother's efforts to redirect her thoughts. The taxi swerved around a streetcar, jolting Elizabeth from her reverie. She glanced at her mother, who gave her a brave smile, though her eyes were misty.

They pulled up to the church as the bells rang out for the nine o'clock Mass. Elizabeth helped her mother from the cab and they joined the stream of churchgoers.

The cavernous interior enveloped them in candlelight and hushed voices. As Elizabeth slid into the polished wooden pew, with her necklace dangling in front of her, the bells fell silent. There was only the faint whisper of prayers.

Elizabeth bowed her head, letting the solemn beauty of the church begin to heal her sorrow. She felt her mother's hand grasp hers, a touching link amidst devastating loss.

The priest's homily was even about loss, as if he knew about the passing. "My brothers and sisters, grief can shroud our hearts like the blackest night. But even when loss dims our days, there are points of light if only we open our eyes - the love of family, the compassion of friends, the promise of reuniting someday in our eternal home."

Elizabeth was moved by his words of solace and hope. She whispered a prayer for her Aunt Gracie as well as all those carrying sorrow today.

Afterward, she and her mother walked down the church steps to browse the nearby Findlay Market, leaves crunching under their feet. They chatted about childhood memories of Gracie and their fondest recollections from happier days. Though tinged with sadness, sharing these stories brought comfort and even occasional laughter.

Stepping into Findlay Market, Elizabeth and her mother were immersed in a sensory feast for the eyes, nose, and taste buds. The bustling indoor market had been a Cincinnati institution since 1855.

They wandered past brightly painted stalls overflowing with plump produce - bushels of apples, mounds of oranges, woven baskets spilling over with glossy eggplant and peppers. The smell of fresh flowers mingled with the smoky aroma of cured meats and pungent cheeses.

For lunch, they shared a decadent charcuterie board from one of the cheerfully decorated delis. As they nibbled on succulent cured meats, creamy cheese, olives, and crackers, their conversation turned to reminiscing about trips to Findlay with Aunt Gracie.

"Oh, how she loved perusing those flower stalls," Elizabeth's mother said with a wistful smile. "Remember how she'd pick out the most exotic bouquets?"

Elizabeth grinned. "And she'd always sneak some fresh pastry for us from the bakery. Even though we'd just had a big lunch!" The memories were bittersweet but brought comfort nonetheless.

Bellies full and spirits lifted, the two women strolled the vibrant market, keeping Gracie's vivacious spirit alive in their hearts.

After their lunch, Elizabeth and her mother exited the market and managed to hail a cab. As they climbed inside, her mother turned to her and said, "I have a little surprise for you, darling." she instructed the driver to take them to Ault Park.

Elizabeth gazed out the window as the cab wound its way up, passing the Mount Lookout Observatory. They drove through a resplendent tunnel of autumn leaves in vibrant hues of crimson, gold, and amber.

When they arrived at the park's overlook, Elizabeth gasped. Spread out before them was an incredible panorama of forests and valleys glowing in the afternoon sunlight. It truly was the crowning jewel of the Queen City.

"Oh Mother, it's breathtaking up here," Elizabeth sighed, squeezing her mother's hand. For a moment, sadness and troubles were blown away by the crisp breeze. There was only sunlit beauty and comforting companionship.

Her mother wrapped an arm around her shoulders. "I hoped you'd like it."

Elizabeth leaned into her mother's embrace, cherishing the memory she had gifted. As the peaceful view stretched before them, she felt Aunt Gracie's spirit at her shoulder.

After admiring the vista from the overlook, Elizabeth and her mother strolled arm-in-arm down into Ault Park proper. Nestled amongst ancient oaks and maples was the park's picturesque pavilion.

The intricate Italian Renaissance-style structure had a peaked roof with a cascading water fountain outside. Arched windows framed views out over the rolling lawns surrounding it. Inside, the majestic ceiling soared.

Elizabeth and her mother sat for a while on a stone bench enjoying the pavilion's cool shade. Elizabeth closed her eyes, soaking in the birdsong and rustling leaves. It was a perfectly peaceful spot to rest and reflect.

When they exited, Elizabeth took one last long look at the graceful building. She imagined ladies and gentlemen of a bygone era gathering there in their finery. For over a century, the pavilion had welcomed generations seeking nature's beauty. She felt blessed to now be among them.

With the pavilion watching over them, Elizabeth and her mother strolled the curving pathways, both longing to linger in this serene place. But the setting sun warned it was time to continue on.

All too soon, Elizabeth and her mother were back in the taxi winding their way down Mount Lookout. After collecting Elizabeth's suitcase from Uncle Herbert's, they continued towards Union Terminal as the gray clouds started to roll in.

When the grand art deco terminal came into view, Elizabeth squeezed her mother's hand tightly. "Thank you for everything, Mother. This was just what I needed."

"Of course, my dear. I'm so glad we had this time together," her mother said, dabbing her eyes. They held each other in a fierce, loving embrace.

"Give Uncle Herbert my love. And let me know about arrangements for Aunt Gracie," Elizabeth said as she pulled away.

Her mother nodded. "She'll be buried in Worthington by her parents, per her wishes. I'll telephone you with the details."

With final goodbyes, Elizabeth passed through the majestic terminal, the awe-inspiring murals lifting her spirits. She was grateful for the bittersweet day honoring Gracie's memory. Holding her loved ones in her heart, she boarded the train back home.

Night had fallen as Elizabeth boarded the train. She settled into her seat as the train lurched into motion. The rhythmic clacking of the wheels over the tracks soon lulled her into a contemplative state.

Muffled conversations mingled with the shuffle of feet and muted thunder of suitcases rolling down the aisle. Rain pattered softly on the windows as autumn fields glided by in darkness.

Lightning flickered, briefly illuminating the shadowy Ohio farmland. As thunder rumbled overhead, Elizabeth felt suddenly cold and alone. She yearned for Samuel's strong arms embracing her, his deep voice gently soothing away her sadness.

In her mind, she replayed their chance encounter at the New England Inn. The intensity of his gaze across the crowded room had awoken long-buried feelings. The memory of his face still thrilled her heart and quickened her pulse.

More than anything, Elizabeth longed to see Samuel again, speak with him, feel his touch. The train sped north through the stormy night as she sat restless, questioning choices that now felt uncertain.

Samuel occupied her thoughts as heavily as the rain lashed the windows. Her longing fused with each crack of thunder echoing her own conflicted heart.

As the train gathered speed, Elizabeth felt her heart racing to match its rapid tempo. The engine's shrill whistle pierced the night as they barreled ahead.

Elizabeth pressed her forehead to the glass, watching her reflection blur with the raindrops streaking down. Her mind blurred too, torn between the past and present.

Seeing Samuel had been like a lightning bolt reanimating dormant feelings. Now her heart galloped as fast as the churning pistons propelling the train forward.

The sway and rumble of the railcar made it impossible to truly rest. Elizabeth shifted in her seat, uneasy with indecision. She sensed she was hurtling towards some unknown reckoning.

Outside, wind-lashed trees whizzed past in ominous shadows. The storm mirrored her inner turbulence. Elizabeth prayed she would find clarity before reaching her destination.

On and on the train plunged through the black rainy night. Mile after mile the train brought her closer to a crossroads she could no longer avoid.

The train began slowing as it approached the outskirts of Northern Columbus. "Next stop, Worthington Station!" the conductor called out. Elizabeth's pulse quickened, knowing she was close to home.

During the ride, her path had become clear. As soon as she dropped her bags, she would head straight for the New England Inn. She had to see Samuel, to demand answers to the questions that plagued her - why he never wrote, where he had been, what brought him back now. The time for confusion was over.

The train grounded to a halt at the tiny station. Rain poured down as Elizabeth stepped onto the platform, the harsh wind whipping her coat. She tightened the belt on her trench coat and unfurled the umbrella her mother gave her before retrieving her suitcase.

Across the tracks, she noticed a small fire flickering under the eaves of the station. There was old Hobo Jeff, hunkered down, wearing a very wet brown jacket cooking a can of beans while taking swigs from a bottle of whiskey.

Elizabeth paused, watching Jeff shiver in the downpour. "I bet he's cold on a night like this," she murmured to herself. But she had no time to delay. With a purposeful stride, Elizabeth hailed a cab and told the driver to drive directly towards the New England Inn with haste.

As they drove on Granville Road to turn south onto High Street, she noticed the rain beginning to let up. Arriving in front of the inn, Elizabeth entered holding her suitcase with her heart pounding. She rushed inside and scanned the bar, but Samuel was nowhere to be found.

Crestfallen and still wet, she hurried to the front desk. "Excuse me, is there a Samuel Lewis staying here?" she asked the attendant breathlessly.

"I'm afraid not, miss," he replied with an apologetic smile. "A Mr. Lewis checked out last evening."

Elizabeth hurried back outside, dismayed. By chance, her cab was still idling by the curb. As she slid despondently into the backseat, the driver gave her a sympathetic look in the rearview mirror.

"No luck finding who you were looking for, miss?" he asked kindly.

"No, I was too late," Elizabeth sighed.

The cabbie clucked his tongue and drove her home. The rain was only sprinkling but drops of water rolled down the street like tears. When they arrived, Elizabeth paid the cabbie and trudged up the puddled driveway, defeated.

But peeking from her mailbox was a letter bearing Samuel's unmistakable handwriting! Heart racing anew, she grabbed the envelope and rushed inside, shutting out the stormy darkness.

With trembling hands, she tore open the seal by the entryway light. Without even shutting the front door, a thrill of anticipation ran through her as she rapidly scanned the letter's contents, hungry for answers at last.

Elizabeth turned on the hallway light and eagerly began reading Samuel's letter:

"Dearest Elizabeth,

I'm writing in hopes this letter finds you well. I know it's been many years since we last spoke, and for that, I am deeply sorry. After high school, trying to work the family farm in Kansas during those long, hard years of dust storms took everything I had. I felt it would be too painful to write you when I did not know if or when I might return. I couldn't continue to break your heart or mine.

But now I am back in Worthington. My uncle is training me at his insurance business here. Upon arriving, you were my first thought. That chance glimpse of you at the inn seemed like providence. I regret leaving things unresolved between us for so long. Please know that you have never left my heart.

Your Guy, Samuel"

Tears filled Elizabeth's eyes as she read his heartfelt words. But just then, a chilling scream pierced the night air outside. She dropped the letter and ran to the window. Peering out into the darkness, she struggled to make out the source of the cries.

Squinting into the night, Elizabeth could just make out a male figure wearing a dark trench coat holding what appeared to be an object in his hand. He was sprinting past her house up the street. A minute later, neighbors began emerging from their homes to investigate the commotion.

"What on earth is happening?" came a voice next door. Elizabeth turned to see Betty Whimsfeld stepping outside, robe pulled tight against the chill.

"I'm not sure, I heard a scream and saw someone running," Elizabeth replied. The two women hurried down to the sidewalk, straining to make out details in the darkness.

Soon police car sirens pierced the air. The cars pulled to a stop several houses down, their flashing lights illuminating the street. "That's the Collins' place," Betty exclaimed. "Little Amy's house!"

Elizabeth felt her stomach drop. "Something's wrong, we should go help," she said. Casting one last glance back at Samuel's letter sitting on the table, she rushed with Betty towards the familiar home, praying young Amy was unharmed.

Betty and Elizabeth hurried down the sidewalk toward the Collins' home as a sound of thunder rumbled from the passing storm. The Collins' house windows were ablaze with flashing police lights.

As they got closer, a young officer approached and told the ladies not to approach any further. Through the open front door, they could see Little Amy sitting on her mother's lap, both crying.

Soon the Corbin Funeral Home's Packard-Henney ambulance arrived on the scene. Somber-faced men wheeled out a gurney holding a shrouded figure, Mr. Collins.

Elizabeth could hear one of the police officers telling the ambulance driver, "He was stabbed to death when we got here."

Neighbors lined the street in their robes and slippers, faces pale with shock. "How awful, poor Mr. Collins, he was such a good banker," murmured a shaken Mrs. Reep.

"What on earth happened?" said Mr. Hunter from across the street. His wife dabbed at her eyes with a handkerchief.

"It's Mr. Collins from the Worthington Savings Bank!" replied Mrs. Reep. The puddles on the night street seem to catch the tears of the neighborhood.

Elizabeth gripped Betty's hand tightly, relief washing over her that Amy was unharmed. But the tragedy of Mr. Collins' death still hung heavy in the air as fog started to roll in, leaving the neighborhood reeling.

Betty said, "That sweet little Amy Collins without her father. It's too awful."

Chapter 5: Fog of Confusion

"Elizabeth dear, you must be in shock. Why don't you come stay with me tonight?" Betty offered kindly.

With the fog rolling in and too rattled to decline, Elizabeth allowed herself to be led next door. Inside, Betty's home was cozy and smelled faintly of lavender.

Over steaming mugs of chamomile tea, the women tried to process the night's events. "I just can't wrap my head around it. Poor Mr. Collins," Elizabeth murmured, staring into her tea.

Betty patted her hand. "I know, it's all so senseless. But we'll get through this together."

Both exhausted, Betty walked Elizabeth to the guest room. Looking around, Elizabeth noticed several framed photographs decorating the walls and side table.

Most were pictures of Betty's late husband, Harold. There was one of him as a smiling young newlywed with his arm around a radiant, youthful Betty on their wedding day. Another showed him in his British Navy uniform, looking dashing yet somber.

"Your husband must have had quite a life." said Elizabeth.

"Yes, Harold was from England. We met when I was a nurse stationed there during the Great War. He couldn't stop coming into the hospital to see me. He was a wonderful man. Even though he has been gone for six years now, I still miss him deeply. He's still here with me, though." Betty said, smiling.

The more recent photos depicted Harold in his twilight years - posing proudly next to a fishing haul, laughing with Betty on the porch swing, dozing in his armchair. Each picture captured memories from a long, happy marriage.

On the nightstand was a photo of Betty and Harold together on vacation, leaning into one another affectionately in front of a scenic mountain vista. Though Harold was gone, the room still held his comforting presence.

Looking at the chronicle of photos, Elizabeth felt an acute sense of longing. Seeing Betty and Harold's enduring love strengthened her resolve to reconcile with Samuel before time ran out.

Elizabeth wished Betty a goodnight and headed into the guest room. She pulled the covers up and got into the old bed. She drifted off to the steady tick of the grandfather clock in the hall.

Monday morning came abruptly with the raucous cuckoo bursting from the bedside clock. It was 6 A.M. Elizabeth groggily sat up in the unfamiliar room, the horrible events of last night came flooding back.

Elizabeth quietly let herself out of Betty's guest room. Looking down at the Collins' house, she saw police still milling about.

At home, she washed up and dressed for school in a somber gray dress. The walk to work felt different - subdued and uneasy.

In class, the students were uncharacteristically quiet. Amy's empty desk glaringly obvious. Elizabeth overheard hushed exchanges between students:

"Do you think she's very sad?"

"My ma said her pa died last night."

"What happened to him?"

Before Elizabeth could intervene, Principal Gentry knocked and entered, his face grim. "Children, I'm afraid we have some very upsetting news..."

He went on to gently inform them of Mr. Collins' sudden passing. The students listened wide-eyed, some beginning to weep. Elizabeth's heart broke for young Amy and all the innocent lives upended by this tragedy.

Elizabeth walked home and called her mother.

"Mr. Collins murdered?" Elizabeth's mother said. "Oh dear, that is horrible. Have they made an arrest?"

"Not, that I know of," Elizabeth answered.

"Well, be careful sweetheart, that isn't like Worthington."

"Ok, Mother," Elizabeth replied.

"By the way, Aunt Gracie's funeral will be this Saturday at Walnut Grove Cemetery. The service will be at St. Joseph Cathedral in downtown Columbus. I will mail you the details. Love you sweetheart."

"Love you too, mother." sighed Elizabeth.

Elizabeth then walked up the street to the Lady Alice Beauty Salon, located at 693 ½ High Street, for her hair appointment with Jane.

The salon was abuzz with chatter about the shocking murder as Elizabeth sat in Jane's styling chair.

"I heard that poor Mr. Collins was stabbed and stumbled inside the house and was dead before he hit the floor," said Clara, the manicurist, in a hushed voice.

Jane clicked her tongue as she massaged Elizabeth's scalp. "They say his wife came home to find him lying in a pool of blood! Killed with his kitchen knife. Can you imagine? I'd have swooned dead away."

"This is the biggest thing to happen in Worthington since the Spirit of Columbus airplane landed on High Street back in 28!" another woman said.

"Do they know for certain it was that vagrant, Hobo Jeff?" asked Pearl, waving her pin curls under the dryer hood.

"That's what the police are saying," Jane replied, rinsing the shampoo from Elizabeth's hair.

Elizabeth sat quietly as the women speculated, her mind churning.

"Hobo Jeff," she thought, "He was across town during the time of the Collins murder. It doesn't seem to add up right."

All around the salon, hair dryers roared like airplane engines, punctuated by the click of scissors and a waft of pungent perming solution.

Jane then said, "Mayor Henderson is going to make an address at the Jones Building tonight at 7. Are you going to go, Elizabeth?"

"I think that would be a good idea," Elizabeth answered.

"Oh, by the way, who was that handsome man you were staring at the New England Inn the other night?" asked Jane.

Annoyed, Elizabeth replied, "He's no one!"

"Well, you certainly had your eye on him. Maybe you should try out the new fragrance we just received. It's called Chantilly by Houbigant. It's named after the French lace," Jane said with a wink.

"No thank you, Jane. I'm an engaged woman!" said Elizabeth, shaking her head.

After leaving the salon, Elizabeth walked slowly back home, chilled to the bone. She shivered, unsure if it was from the cold wind or the pall of violence that had descended so unexpectedly upon her peaceful community. As she approached her house, she was startled to see George's motorcycle on the driveway and George waiting on the front steps, hat in hand.

"Elizabeth! I came as soon as I heard the terrible news," he said, rushing to meet her.

"Are you alright? This is just ghastly business with Mr. Collins. And poor Amy without a father now..." George trailed off, shaking his head.

"I'm still in shock," Elizabeth replied. "It's all so unreal."

George gripped her hand tightly. "Well don't you worry, I'm here now. We'll move up the wedding date, and get you safely out of this dreadful place. I won't have my betrothed living alone with a killer on the loose."

Elizabeth bit her tongue. She knew George meant well, but his immediate insistence on accelerating wedding plans irked her. There were much deeper wounds here than could be solved by a rushed marriage of convenience.

Seeing her weary expression, George softened. "Forgive me, you've been through an ordeal. Get inside and rest, my dear. We'll talk more tomorrow." He squeezed her hand and left on his motorbike.

Elizabeth watched him go with conflicted feelings before heading inside at last.

Exhausted, she started preparing dinner for herself before the mayor's address. As she was washing vegetables, a knock sounded at the front door.

"George again," she thought with an impatient huff, drying her hands to answer it. But when she opened the door, it was Samuel standing before her, face etched with concern.

"Samuel!" Elizabeth gasped, suddenly lightheaded.

"Elizabeth, forgive me for just showing up like this. I came as soon as I heard about Mr. Collins," he said, words rushing out. "I had to make sure you were all right."

Elizabeth stood frozen for a moment, pulse racing. Then, before she could think, she stepped forward and embraced him, all the tumultuous emotions of the past few days spilling over.

Samuel stiffened in surprise before wrapping his arms around her. "Shhh, it's okay. I'm here now." he murmured soothingly.

When her tears had subsided, Elizabeth felt angered. She pushed him away.

"You didn't even bother to write or call after all those years!" she yelled.

"Elizabeth, sweetheart, it was the Great Depression. I didn't know if I would ever be back. There was no use trying to hold onto something when I had no hope. I wanted you to go find a guy you liked, not waste your time waiting for me. That would have been unfair and selfish of me to try and make you hold on."

Samuel embraced Elizabeth, overcome with emotion.

"I'm also sorry to hear about your father's passing. My uncle told me." said Samuel.

"There have been a lot of changes, Samuel, since you were here. It's been five years!" replied Elizabeth almost in tears.

"You're also a teacher?" asked Samuel.

"Yes, I've been teaching for a few years now," replied Elizabeth as her mind was racing with thoughts.

"And your mother?" asked Samuel.

"She went down to Cincinnati when my Aunt Gracie got sick. My aunt just passed away," said Elizabeth.

"I'm sorry to hear that, too." Samuel replied as he stared deep into her eyes.

After a few moments of silence, Elizabeth mentioned that she needed to get to the mayor's address soon.

"Yes, you should go hear what the mayor says. But can we talk more after?" Elizabeth nodded, dabbing her eyes.

Just then, Betty appeared on the sidewalk. "Oh Elizabeth, I was just coming to walk with you..." she stopped short, seeing Samuel.

"Well, I'll be! If it isn't Samuel Lewis back in Worthington!" Betty exclaimed. Turning to Elizabeth with a knowing smile she added, "We can all walk to the Jone's building together."

"The Jone's Building?" questioned Samuel.

"Oh, that's where the village leases a room until we can get a proper town hall building." replied Betty.

The three walked up New England Avenue. Betty pointed out a slanted brick house south of the New England Inn.

"That's the Snow House, Samuel. I don't know if you remember the Snow family, but they recently moved out." said Betty.

"I didn't know them but I know the family was active in the Masons." Samuel replied.

Betty kept up cheerful chatter, allowing Elizabeth and Samuel to walk in thoughtful silence, hands brushing occasionally. The Jone's building was located just south of the Red and White. They walked up to the second floor. The familiar warmth of his presence buoyed Elizabeth's spirits as they hurried to get answers about the shadow over the village.

The building was overflowing with somber residents hoping for answers. Elizabeth, Samuel, and Betty shuffled into cramped into chairs as Mayor Henderson took the podium standing next to Police Chief Engel and Officer Jameson.

The wood-paneled hall featured flags and patriotic bunting framing the stage. The paintings, hung on the wall depicting Worthington's history, glowed in the evening light. Despite the grandeur, an uneasy atmosphere permeated the space.

Mayor Henderson held up his hands for quiet. His round face was uncharacteristically grave as he prepared to address the crowded room.

"My friends, this is a dark time for our fair village," he began heavily. "As you all know, Worthington lost one of its own last night in a truly reprehensible act of violence against banker Mr. Frank Collins."

Police Chief Engel nodded his head as he stood beside the mayor in the crowded room. Murmurs rose from the audience as the mayor described what was known about the stabbing. The mayor stated that Jeff, the village vagrant, was in custody and that police believe it was a robbery gone bad. But the investigation was ongoing. Offering his condolences to the Collins family, he along and Chief Engel vowed to pursue justice tirelessly.

As Elizabeth listened, she noticed details still didn't quite make sense. She saw Hobo Jeff outside of Worthington Station eating in the rain shortly before the murder. He was a drunk but he never tended towards violence. Besides, it would have taken him at least 25 minutes to walk to the other side of town to get to Collins house. He never had money for a cab and he definitely was not a good sprinter.

When the mayor finished his speech, polite applause echoed through the hall. But a current of unease remained palpable.

Worthington's peace had been broken, and it would be a long road back to normalcy.

As the crowd filtered out of town hall, Elizabeth spotted George waiting by the steps, his face like a storm cloud. Before she could react, he strode towards them.

"Elizabeth! What is the meaning of this?" George demanded, glaring at Samuel. "I thought I made my feelings about this rascal clear long ago."

"Good to see you too George! It's been a long time since high school," commented Samuel.

George bristled but Elizabeth stepped between them. "George, please, Samuel is just accompanying me as a friend. Can we not do this now?"

"Absolutely not!" George fumed. "I arrive to comfort my bride-to-be and find she's fraternizing with riff-raff from her past. I won't stand for it!"

The two men looked about ready to come to blows. Flustered, Betty tried to calm the situation but George refused to listen.

"Mark my words, Elizabeth, consorting with this vagabond will only lead to your ruin," George spat. "And you, Samuel, go back out west to your dust bowl!" George yelled as he stormed off.

Elizabeth stood trembling, Samuel gripping her hand supportively. Betty offered an apologetic look. "Dear me, let's get you home. That George is nothing but trouble."

After the tense encounter, Samuel tried lightening the mood by inviting Elizabeth and Betty for a drink at the New England Inn. But Elizabeth demurred, the evening's drama having sapped her energy.

"I should be getting home. It's been quite a day," she said wearily.

"Let me walk you ladies at least," Samuel offered. Elizabeth nodded gratefully and the three ambled down New England Avenue.

At Elizabeth's door, Samuel took her hands gently. "I know there's much we need to discuss. Can we meet tomorrow evening? I can stop by again." Elizabeth managed a small smile. "Of course."

Samuel smiled back, the familiar warmth reaching his eyes. "It will be wonderful to truly talk again. Get some rest, Elizabeth."

The two embraced as Betty looked on smiling.

"Good night, ladies!" Samuel said just before he walked down the driveway.

After he departed, Betty hooked her arm through Elizabeth's. "Come have some cocoa dear, soothe your nerves after all this excitement." Elizabeth readily agreed, craving her wise neighbor's soothing presence.

The two women soon sat cradling mugs in Betty's cozy kitchen, contemplating the day's dramatic events. Stirring her cocoa, Elizabeth suddenly remembered another important detail from the night of the murder.

"Betty, there's something else. Right after I heard the awful scream, I saw someone running up the street. A shadowy figure all in black. There was an object in his hand."

Betty's eyes widened. "Is that so? Well, that's highly significant! Do you think it was Hobo Jeff?"

Elizabeth shook her head. "No, I had just seen Hobo Jeff at Worthington Station. He wasn't wearing a dark trench coat like this guy. Now that I think about it, it was definitely someone fleeing the scene."

"You must tell Officer Jameson immediately," Betty advised. "Not just about Hobo Jeff's whereabouts, but this mysterious stranger you witnessed. It could break the case wide open!"

"You're right," Elizabeth agreed, feeling energized by this new lead. "First thing tomorrow I'll go straight to Jameson and tell him everything. If I can cast doubt on Jeff's guilt, maybe they'll look closer at other suspects."

The two women stayed up late into the night piecing together clues and trying to make sense of the baffling crime that had shaken their quiet village.

As their empty mugs grew cold, Betty's eyes took on a gleam of determination. "If you want to get to the bottom of this, I'd be happy to help investigate."

She rushed to the closet and emerged with a sturdy metal flashlight. "We can be like detectives - Holmes and Watson!" Betty declared, switching on the light and holding it under her chin like a villain in a movie drama.

Elizabeth couldn't help but giggle at her eccentric neighbor's antics. "Alright Detective Betty, you're on the case," she said lightheartedly.

Bidding her partner goodnight, Elizabeth walked back home feeling buoyed. But a chill swept over her as she saw the Collins' dark, shuttered house. The killer was still out there somewhere.

She shivered and hurried inside, reassured that their little makeshift detective squad would uncover the truth and restore order in Worthington once more.

On Tuesday morning, Elizabeth hurried to the police station, determined to share her eyewitness account. She was shown to Officer Jameson's desk right away.

Elizabeth described seeing a mysterious figure fleeing up the street just after the scream pierced the night. Jameson listened intently, scribbling notes.

"That's quite curious, ma'am, but we remain certain we've got the culprit," Jameson said. He explained a bloody knife had been found near Hobo Jeff's shack and identified by Mrs. Collins as theirs.

"I know what I saw," Elizabeth insisted. "And I know Jeff was at the station when it happened, too drunk to make it to the Collins' house. Someone else killed Mr. Collins and planted that knife to frame Jeff!"

But Jameson simply shook his head. "Open and shut case in my book. We'll pass your statement to the chief, but I don't expect it'll change much."

Frustrated, Elizabeth left the station. If the police wouldn't listen, she was more determined than ever to prove Jeff's innocence and bring the real killer to justice.

As Elizabeth turned to leave, Officer Jameson called her back. "Now just a moment, ma'am. The investigation is actually being led by a detective from the Franklin County Sheriff's Office Homicide Unit."

This piqued Elizabeth's interest. "Who is the detective? Could I speak with him?"

Jameson shook his head apologetically. "You'll have to take that up with the chief. But in the meantime, Hobo Jeff is in our temporary holding cell if you want to talk to him."

Eagerly, Elizabeth asked if she could see Jeff right away. Jameson acquiesced and led her back to the cramped cell where a disheveled Jeff sat scowling on the cot.

"You've got a visitor, Jeff. It's Miss Elizabeth Russo." Jameson announced, unlocking the door to the holding area. He lingered by the bars as Elizabeth stood outside the holding cell. Jeff's eyes widened in surprise when he recognized her.

"Miss Russo, you gotta believe me, I didn't kill nobody!" Jeff burst out.

Elizabeth moved closer. "Just tell me what happened Sunday night?" she said gently.

"It was raining something fierce that night," Jeff explained with a faraway look. "I was trying to get a fire going and cook up some beans, but the wood was too wet. Ended up drinking most of my whiskey just to get warm."

He shook his head sadly. "Must've passed out for a spell. When I woke up it was late. Next mornin' the police showed up saying they found a knife outside my place and then I'm arrested for murder!"

Jeff wrung his hands in distress. "But I never left my shack all night, I swear it! And I ain't never seen that knife either. Someone's trying to pin this thing on me real hard."

Elizabeth patted his shoulder. "I believe you, Jeff. We're going to figure out what really happened. Just hang in there."

Leaving the cell, Elizabeth felt even more motivated to uncover the truth. Jeff was a harmless local vagrant, not a violent killer. And she was going to prove it.

After a few more minutes, Officer Jameson said, "Time's up, Miss Russo, I'll have to ask you to leave now."

As Jameson escorted her out, Elizabeth said firmly, "That knife was planted to frame Jeff, I'm sure of it."

Jameson shook his head. "Couldn't be, ma'am. There was only one set of footprints in the mud outside his shack where we found the knife. Those footprints belong to Jeff."

Elizabeth's mind spun as she walked slowly back to school in the unusually warm fall weather. One set of footprints...that seemed to implicate Jeff beyond a doubt. And yet her gut still told her the vagrant was innocent. There had to be an explanation.

Elizabeth was more determined than ever to get to the bottom of this mystery. If only she could fit all the puzzle pieces together, maybe then she'd have answers.

Arriving late for school, Elizabeth found her students uncharacteristically subdued, little Amy's chair still sat empty. The Collins tragedy was weighing heavily on the class. Hoping to lift their spirits, Elizabeth invited Miss Greener's class to join hers for an ice cream outing at lunchtime.

The children's faces immediately brightened at the prospect. As the sun shined, they walked across Granville Road and then High Street eagerly to Birnie's Drug Store for some Telling's Ice Cream. As they walked into the store, the scrumptious smells wafted through the door making their mouths water.

Mike, the man behind the counter, greeted them cheerily, handing out heaping scoops of creamy confections - chocolate, strawberry, pistachio. The kids' joyous chatter rose above the din of the bustling shop.

With treats in hand, they headed to the Village Green to enjoy their cold desserts under the warm autumn sun. As they ate, Danny, the local high schooler who took the photo of the car accident, came by and offered to snap a photo of the classes. The children beamed with sticky-faced delight.

For a moment, the shadow over Worthington lifted. Elizabeth was glad to bring some lightness back to her students' young lives. Their innocence deserved protection.

She savored a lick of sweet vanilla ice cream, bracing herself for the challenges yet to come in uncovering the truth. The children laughed and chatted loudly as they devoured their ice cream cones, drips running down their small hands.

"Oh my, you're all getting so sticky!" Elizabeth exclaimed with amusement. "Miss Greener, could you please pass me a tissue from that Sitroux box?"

"Of course." Miss Greener replied, grabbing the floral-printed box of tissues and handing several to Elizabeth.

Elizabeth gently wiped the dripping ice cream off each child's hands and face, the cherry red stain spreading across the tissues. The kids squirmed but patiently allowed her to clean them up.

"There now, all fresh and tidy again." Elizabeth declared, stuffing the soiled tissues into her pocketbook. The students sprang up to resume playing, invigorated by the treat.

Elizabeth watched them fondly, spirits lifted by their resilient joy. With some ice cream and laughter, they had found a pocket of normalcy again amidst the town's darkness and troubles.

After their sweet respite on the Green, the Worthington Presbyterian Church bells began tolling one o'clock.

"Alright children, time to head back to school," Elizabeth announced, gathering their trash. The resonant gongs echoed down the hillside as they started their walk back.

The students skipped along happily, all sticky traces from their treat gone. Their youthful chatter mingled with the bells' rhythmic peals.

As they crossed Granville Road, the impressive edifice of the school came into view. The bells fell silent as the last child filed back into the building.

Elizabeth watched them fondly as she returned to the classroom, the innocent laughter still ringing in her ears. For now, the darkness that had gripped Worthington retreated to the edges of her mind. But she knew the mysteries remained to be unraveled before peace could fully return.

After school, Elizabeth walked home pensively, thinking about everything that had happened in the past few days. She ate dinner and then sat on the couch to look at the sale numbers from the store. She was hoping to meet Samuel later that night but they hadn't made any concrete plans. Her head was drifting in and out of sleep from being up late the night before. Elizabeth woke up to a knock on the door. As she got up, she looked at the clock. It was already 8:15 P.M. She walked to the front door and opened it. There, stood Samuel holding a bouquet of beautiful flowers.

"These are for you," he said with a smile. "May I come in?"

"Of course. Please, have a seat," Elizabeth replied graciously, ushering him inside. She put the flowers in water and joined him at the kitchen table.

"I spoke with the police and that vagrant Jeff today," she began. "Jeff insists he's innocent and I'm certain he's telling the truth."

She described to Samuel seeing the mysterious fleeing figure after the scream. "It was too late for Jeff to have gotten there; I know it. Someone else killed Mr. Collins and framed Jeff. I just have to prove it."

Samuel nodded thoughtfully. "It does seem suspicious. What can I do to help get to the bottom of this?"

Just as Elizabeth and Samuel were discussing leads, an urgent knock came at the door. Elizabeth opened it to find Betty, flashlight in hand. "I'm ready to investigate!" she declared.

An idea struck Elizabeth. "Let's go examine the area around Worthington Station where Hobo Jeff was that night."

Samuel offered to drive them in his uncle's car that was parked out front. Elizabeth grabbed a pen and notebook and her father's old camera with a flash bulb. Under cover of foggy darkness, they pulled up near the cordoned-off crime scene. When they got out of the car, the sound of a train whistle echoed far away.

Betty's flashlight cut a feeble beam through the gloom as they approached Jeff's ramshackle shelter that he likely assembled from discarded wood from Potter Lumber across the tracks. Samuel shivered next to Elizabeth. "It sure is creepy out here at night."

Elizabeth felt emboldened by his solid presence. "Jeff said he saw a truck speeding off last night. Maybe we can find tire prints."

Betty swung her flashlight beam over the dark, foggy ground surrounding the shack. As it swept across the muddy earth, the light glinted off some deep ruts.

"Look there!" Elizabeth exclaimed, rushing over. Crouching down, she saw clearly that they were tire tracks indented into the mud a few feet from the shack.

"Just as Jeff described, a vehicle was here that night," she said excitedly. Samuel nodded, peering at the tracks closely.

Elizabeth quickly dug her father's camera out of her bag. She carefully positioned it above the tire tracks and popped the flash bulb, capturing the evidence on film.

"This is proof that Hobo Jeff was telling the truth about seeing a truck speeding off," Elizabeth said.

"Let's follow the mud tracks to see where it leads," replied Betty.

The three followed the tire tracks, which led towards Granville Road.

Their hearts raced as fast as the vehicle that had been here. The photo felt like the first step in finding a smoking gun supporting Jeff's innocence. Justice and truth were within their grasp.

Just as they turned to leave, a loud voice shouted "Hey, you!" They whirled around to see Milkman Bailey approaching, looking stern out of uniform.

"That's an active crime scene, best you folks stay away," he scolded. They murmured apologies and hurried back towards the car.

Samuel whispered, "Guess we'd better skedaddle before Sherlock Bones here cracks the case." Despite everything, Elizabeth had to stifle a grin.

Safely in the car, their pulses raced as they sped away into the night. Samuel dropped Betty off with thanks for her help.

Alone with Samuel in the moonlight, Elizabeth felt suddenly self-conscious. At her door, he gazed at her intently. "Aren't you going to invite me in?"

She hesitated, flustered. "It's rather late. And I am still an engaged woman after all."

Samuel looked disappointed but simply squeezed her hand. "You're right, Elizabeth, but there's just something about you."

Just then Samuel embraced Elizabeth and bent his head down to kiss her. Elizabeth moved her head out of the way to avoid the kiss but then moved back in front of Samuel. Their lips touched and they shared a deep passionate moment. She then pushed him away.

"Sam, I can't, I can't do this. That's a bad idea. Goodnight."

Samuel stood quietly and began to walk to the car.

Elizabeth closed the front door and leaned against it, her mind spinning. The brief kiss from Samuel had awakened a torrent of emotions within her - confusion, exhilaration, longing, and also fear.

Fear of what these feelings meant, now that she had pledged herself to another man.

She touched her lips, still tingling from the tender yet fleeting contact. It had been just a small moment of affection, and yet it threatened to disrupt everything Elizabeth thought she wanted in life.

Pushing off from the door, Elizabeth busied herself getting ready for bed, attempting to ignore the cauldron of emotions bubbling inside. But as she lay staring up at the ceiling, images of Samuel kept intruding on thoughts of her dutiful fiancé, George.

Seeking comfort, Elizabeth reached up and clutched the necklace Aunt Gracie had gifted her. She could almost feel her aunt's soothing presence as she rubbed her thumb over the pendant. She could almost see Aunt Gracie again.

"Oh, Aunt Gracie, I wish you were here to advise me," Elizabeth whispered into the darkness. A single tear slipped down her cheek as she continued holding tight to the keepsake.

Elizabeth replayed Gracie's words of wisdom in her mind: "Follow where your heart leads you." Her heart yearned for Samuel, yet duty and obligation pulled her towards George. The opposing forces battled within her.

Gripping the necklace like a talisman, Elizabeth prayed for strength and discernment. She trusted in time, the confusing fog of emotions would lift, revealing the way forward. For now, she drew comfort from Gracie's gift and the love it represented. Finally, exhausted, Elizabeth drifted off to sleep.

Chapter 6: Disturbance in the Grove

Elizabeth awoke early to turn on the stove to heat water for the tea. She was hoping it would soothe her conflicted thoughts. She could still feel Samuel's lips pressed upon hers. The autumn chill was setting in, leaves transforming into dazzling hues outside her window. The swirl of the leaves and her emotions lingered and Halloween would be here before they knew it.

The kettle full of water started to warm up. A faint whisper of steam began rising as the metal base slowly heated. The kettle rattled softly.

Gradually the noises grew louder. Just as the kettle began emitting a high-pitched whistle, a sudden thud on the front porch made Elizabeth jump.

She rushed to the window and peeked out. There was the milkman, Mr. Bailey, placing the bottles on her steps briskly before climbing into his idling Gabel Dairy milk truck. Elizabeth watched as he pulled away with a little wave. She opened the front door to find the fresh milk bottles on the step, condensation already beading on the glass. She reached down to grab the milk bottles and the morning paper.

Glancing up, she spotted Mr. Bailey down the street in his delivery truck. The rear wheels on the driver's side were caked with mud. Something about the milkman's truck didn't sit right.

The kettle was now screeching insistently. Elizabeth hurried to pull it from the burner before the whistle became ear-splitting. As she poured the steaming water into her teacup, she resolved to tell Betty about the odd observation.

Elizabeth thought back to the previous night at the Worthington Station. Milkman Bailey had crept up on them unexpectedly while they were investigating. She shivered slightly, recalling the eerie encounter.

As she sat down at the kitchen table, Elizabeth added a splash of milk and a dash of sugar to her tea. She would have to keep an eye on the over-eager milkman. His muddy tires suggested he too may have visited the crime scene recently.

Sipping the hot drink, Elizabeth steeled herself for another day of unraveling Worthington's mystery. But before doing that, she had to browse the Worthington newspaper. Sipping her tea, Elizabeth unfolded the morning paper. The front page bore a solemn headline: "Banker Collins to Be Laid to Rest Today, Suspected Killer Arrested". It noted that Mr. Collins was survived by his wife and daughter, and donations could be made to support the grieving family.

Setting down the paper, Elizabeth telephoned Worthington Cabs to request a ride to the cemetery. She had decided to pay her respects at Gracie's burial site this morning and to meet her uncle and mother there before the funeral service.

Donning a black dress, the necklace Aunt Gracie gave to her, and a jacket, Elizabeth locked up and climbed into the waiting taxi. The ride to Walnut Grove Cemetery was silent, giving her time to collect her thoughts. When they arrived at the cemetery's wrought iron gates, Elizabeth could see the mourners gathered outside for Mr. Collins's funeral. Elizabeth quietly got out of the cab away from the gathering and tipped her driver a quarter.

As she walked slowly past the Collins' service, she offered a silent prayer for the struggling family. Even though she did not see eye to eye with Mrs. Collins, she would never wish anything like what they experienced for any family. As Elizabeth walked past the gathering for

Mr. Collins, little Amy suddenly broke from her mother and ran over to her. Despite the somber setting, Amy was grinning ear to ear.

"Miss Russo! Miss Russo! Dr. Bently says he's taking me and mother to Hollywood so I can become a movie star!" she exclaimed breathlessly.

Elizabeth masked her surprise, simply replying "How nice for you, dear." In truth, she found it odd that the wealthy Dr. Bently, the village's physician, had suddenly taken such an interest in the Collins family. Perhaps, though, he was trying to help them as they grieved.

Just then, Mrs. Collins noticed Amy's absence and hurried over, scolding her back to the funeral party. Elizabeth offered a polite nod before continuing. She walked further into the older circle part of the cemetery. The trees were larger and there were people buried there as far back as the War of 1812. Every Decoration Day the parade ended up in that section where a tribute was made to the fallen soldiers who gave the ultimate sacrifice to the country. The leaves covered the ground with a beautiful array of colors. Aunt Gracie could not have had a more beautiful day to be buried in the cemetery.

"Elizabeth!" called her mother from a distance. Elizabeth raised her head and saw her mother standing with Uncle Herbert underneath a grand oak tree. They wanted to meet in the cemetery to inspect the gravesite before the church service and burial. Elizabeth greeted both of them with a hug. There was a glance of sadness from Uncle Herbert, but when he stepped back to look at Elizabeth a large smile appeared on his face.

"You wore your aunt's necklace. She would have been thrilled," he said. The three of them held hands and shared a moment of silence for Gracie. It was enough to give them the energy to make it to the church service.

"Alright ladies, we have an appointment to keep," said Uncle Herb as he motioned the two to the opened doors of his Studebaker. He drove them to downtown Columbus' St. Joseph Cathedral for the service. The church bells rang as they pulled past the hearse funeral car waiting out front. They turned into the cathedral parking lot.

As the three of them walked in, the organ swelled inside the church. The sounds of her mother and Elizabeth's high-heeled shoes sounded on top of the granite floor. As they walked up to the front pew, people came up to greet them. Far more people showed up for the service than Elizabeth anticipated. Though Gracie had grown up in Worthington, it had been several decades since she moved to Cincinnati to live with Herb before the Great Depression. She still had a lot of high school friends in town and many made the trek up from the Cincinnati suburb, Price Hill. It was her intention to be buried in Walnut Grove alongside her parents. Herb wanted her happy and got a plot next to hers.

Elizabeth sat with her mother and Uncle Herbert in the quiet church, absently rubbing Gracie's necklace between her fingers.

"Gracie would be so touched to see you wearing that," her mother whispered. Elizabeth nodded, a lump forming in her throat.

Suddenly, the solemn silence was pierced by the roar of a motorcycle pulling up outside. The doors creaked open and heavy footsteps echoed down the aisle. There was George, clad in a black leather jacket.

"Apologies for my late arrival," he muttered, squeezing in next to a dismayed Elizabeth.

As the opening hymn began, Elizabeth glanced back and spotted Samuel standing respectfully in the rear pew. Their eyes met briefly and he gave a small nod of understanding.

The priest began the mass with a brief prayer about life's fragility and the hope of everlasting peace. "Though Gracie has left this earth, her spirit will live on in our hearts and memories," he proclaimed.

The brilliant sunlight streaming through the stained glass splashed color around the church, as if Gracie's vigor was there among them.

Elizabeth was profoundly comforted imagining her aunt at rest in a beautiful realm beyond this world.

After the moving service, the funeral procession wound its way back to Walnut Grove Cemetery. Leaves in brilliant hues of red and gold drifted down from the trees as if nature's confetti was bidding Gracie farewell.

At the graveside, the casket was gently lowered as voices raised in the poignant strains of "Amazing Grace" a fitting tribute to Aunt Gracie's beautiful spirit. Elizabeth shed cathartic tears, her mother squeezing her hand supportively.

Back home, Elizabeth and her mother prepared a buffet supper for family members. Roasted turkey with sage dressing, sweet potato casserole, green beans, and warm buttery rolls with jam. Gracie's favorite foods filled the house with comforting aromas.

They shared memories and comforted one another late into the evening. Though Gracie was gone, her vivacious imprint on their hearts remained.

After the guests and George had departed, Elizabeth turned to her mother. "When do you think you'll come back to Worthington now that Gracie has passed?"

Her mother paused thoughtfully. "Dear, after six months I've decided to remain in Cincinnati. I'm quite content there my bridge club friends, the Catholic parish I've joined, and Uncle Herbert nearby."

Elizabeth was taken aback. "But what about the house here?"

"Well, you and George will need it to start a family!" her mother replied matter-of-factly. "I'm looking forward to visiting my future grandkids often."

Elizabeth felt uneasy at this presumption. In all the chaos, she had scarcely thought about having children with George. The idea no longer held the same appeal as it once did.

"We'll see about that mother. Let's get through the wedding first," Elizabeth answered carefully. Her mother simply smiled and squeezed her hand, lost in rosy visions of the future.

But privately, Elizabeth harbored growing doubts about the path to which she had committed. The possibilities from here seemed far less clear.

After an emotionally draining day, Elizabeth bid her mother goodnight. Alone in her bedroom, Elizabeth's mind spun with the day's events.

She kept returning to little Amy Collins' claim that Dr. Bently planned to whisk them away to Hollywood and stardom. It made no sense. Bently was a reclusive doctor, not an entertainment mogul. Where were these extravagant promises coming from? And how did he have the means after the Depression had ravaged so many fortunes?

As exhaustion overtook her, Elizabeth's racing thoughts blurred into hazy dreams where she saw her Aunt Gracie. She turned to her with a warm smile. "You are always a wonderful niece," she laughed lightly. "I miss you, Aunt Gracie, I wish I knew what to do."

She squeezed Elizabeth's hand. Her face grew serious. "Elizabeth, your place is to fight for truth and justice. There is darkness to be conquered in Worthington. There is something dirty going on!" Her image began fading into fog as Elizabeth called out "Wait, what do you mean?"

Elizabeth awoke with a start, pale moonlight filtering through the curtains. Her aunt's words lingered like the perfume of a woman who had recently left a building. Elizabeth thought of the shadowy figure fleeing the Collins' home - the key to unraveling this mystery. If only she could expose whoever it was running past her house.

Morning came too soon, her mother rapping on the door. "Rise and shine, Sunday morning, time to get ready for church!" Elizabeth rubbed her eyes and slowly dressed; body weary but spirit restless.

She needed to speak with Samuel and Betty about their amateur investigation.

After the Sunday church service, where Elizabeth spent more time daydreaming than praying, she declined to join her family for brunch. "I should prepare my lessons for tomorrow," she told her mother. There was a flash of disappointment, but no argument. She hugged her mother and Uncle Herbert and wished them a safe trip back to Cincinnati.

Finally, alone again, Elizabeth changed into practical pants and a shirt, pinning up her hair. No more distractions. Today she would uncover new clues, she could feel it. The necklace from Aunt Gracie seemed to glow from where it lay on her dresser.

"Wish me luck, Gracie," Elizabeth whispered. She imagined her aunt waving encouragement as she set off purposefully into the heart of town.

The main street bustled with churchgoers socializing after services. Elizabeth nodded politely and waited on the Village Green, just outside of the Worthington Presbyterian Church. She hoped she might catch Samuel coming out from the Sunday service.

Moments later he appeared walking outside with his aunt and uncle, brow knitted in concern. He walked over towards Elizabeth.

"Elizabeth? Has something happened?" asked Samuel.

Elizabeth smiled reassuringly. "Nothing new. But we need to meet with Betty and compare notes. Loose ends need to be tied up."

Samuel, looking concerned, then said, "You remember my Uncle Howard and my Aunt Rosemary?"

"How do you do, Elizabeth? Wonderful to see you again," replied Uncle Howard

"Good to see you again, sir," Elizabeth nodded.

Samuel visibly relaxed. "Of course. Let me fetch my coat and we'll go call on her." Elizabeth waited impatiently as he hurried to his uncle's car. Their investigation had idled too long. New energy coursed through Elizabeth, propelling her forward.

Elizabeth and Samuel walked to Betty's house. The door swung open after a few brisk knocks. "Well, it's about time you two! Here I was starting to think I'd have to solve this mystery solo," she exclaimed, ushering them inside.

Over strong black tea, they pooled their knowledge so far about the baffling murder. "We know Hobo Jeff is innocent, but can't prove it," Elizabeth recounted. Betty chimed in "And the police are dead certain they've got their man."

Samuel had been quiet but now spoke up. "Well, did you think of any other clues from Worthington Station? The guy that yelled at us there the other night was nuts!" Elizabeth nodded vigorously and thought about the dream she had last night. Aunt Gracie said there was something dirty going on. That's it, the milk truck!

"He seemed eager to keep us away from that area. And this morning when he dropped off my milk, his rear wheels were caked in mud." Elizabeth added gravely, "Might be nothing, but seems worth investigating his movements that night."

Betty leaped up. "Well, what are we waiting for? Let's go visit him. I still have that flashlight if we need to do some sneaking." She headed for the door before they could respond.

Elizabeth exchanged an amused glance with Samuel. Impulsive as ever, Betty had the right spirit. Elizabeth went into her bedroom and grabbed her father's camera, flash bulb and all. They hurried after her out into the crisp afternoon.

The Gabel Dairy Milk depot was east of the village near Worthington Station. The trio hailed a Worthington cab on High Street. The cab then turned right on Granville Road.

As they drove past the residential streets, families could be glimpsed through front windows enjoying luncheons and card games. At one home, a father swung his laughing daughter high in the air, while the mother looked on tenderly. Elizabeth felt a pang watching the carefree scene.

The further the cab drove from the village center, the more dilapidated the buildings became. The Gabel Dairy Milk depot was in a grubby warehouse district by the railway tracks. "Remind me why we go this way again?" Samuel asked wryly, shivering against the chill wind.

Betty shushed him as the cab dropped them off outside the depot's faded green loading doors. "Let me do the talking," she whispered before hammering on the metal with a gloved fist. The sound reverberated emptily within.

Just as Betty was gearing up to pound again, the door creaked open a sliver. A gray-haired man peered out suspiciously. "Can I help you folks?" he asked in a gravelly voice.

"Good day, sir. We were hoping to have a word with Mr. Bailey if he's on the premises," Betty replied brightly. The man's eyes narrowed further. "And what might this be concerning?"

Betty improvised hastily. "Well, my two friends here are newlyweds, just moved to town. They wanted to start up milk delivery but forgot to ask Mr. Bailey about his business hours for new customers."

Elizabeth froze at the words "newlyweds" but Samuel smoothly slipped an arm around her. "Yes indeed, just hitched last month! But the missus here plumb forgot to get the milkman's schedule for our new home," he said with an exaggerated drawl and dopey grin.

The gray haired man replied, "You'd have to ask him yourself. Do you want to have him give you a call?"

"No, we can send him a letter. Do you happen to know where he lives?" asked Betty.

"Oh, he lives down by the river just past the high school on the other side of Granville Road. Just look for the Gabel Dairy Milk truck."

"Will do, thank you, sir," replied Samuel. The trio hailed a taxi back to Elizabeth's house.

Nightfall provided the perfect cover as Betty, Samuel, and Elizabeth set out towards Milkman Bailey's home on the edge of town towards the Olentangy River. Elizabeth brought her father's camera and Aunt Gracie's necklace for luck, Samuel carried the notepad, while Betty brandished her flashlight like a saber.

"Remember, quiet as church mice," Betty whispered loudly as they crept up to Bailey's truck, parked in the drive. The caked mud was still evident on the rear wheels. As they got close to the house, the blinds were pulled down but the lights were on. On the second floor, they could see the shadows of two people silhouetted behind the blinds. As they got closer, they could hear what sounded like men arguing.

"I want my money!" one man was overheard shouting. "I've got your check right here, Bailey!" another man answered.

They didn't want to come anywhere close to the house but, Samuel was scribbling in the notebook while Betty was illuminating it with her flashlight. Elizabeth just wanted a photo of the milk truck, the driver-side muddy tires, and the rear passenger-side tire with no mud.

Elizabeth slowly circled the vehicle, camera at the ready. She could see the mud still there not just on the rear driver-side tire, but also on the front driver-side tire. She focused first on the driver-side muddy tires. The brilliant flash momentarily illuminated the yard. The men in the house still could be heard arguing. Elizabeth focused her camera on a distinct zig-zag tread pattern imprinted on the tire without mud. With a silent prayer, she pressed the shutter button.

Shielding her eyes from the glare, Betty pointed to the truck's side panel. "Get the make and model too on that tire! We need proof it's Bailey's rig." Nodding, Elizabeth waited for the spots to clear from her vision before taking another blinding shot of the truck details.

Samuel wrote the specifics in a small notebook to corroborate the photographic evidence. Their hearts pounded, pulses racing faster than the time it took to reload the camera flash.

"Nice job, my star investigative team!" Samuel joked. But the raised voices carried in the still night. Suddenly, the sounds of the blinds quickly rolling up and the interior lights of the house encompassed the front lawn.

"Who's out there!" yelled a man from inside the house.

"Run!" Samuel yelled. The trio sprinted off as the front door slammed open behind them. They didn't dare glance back as they raced for the sanctuary of darkness.

The two ladies ran following Samuel.

"We can't go towards downtown, whoever that was will see us. We'll have to hide in the woods. Go towards the river." said Samuel.

Only when they ran into the woods, moon aglow, did they finally stop, gasping to catch their breath. Peals of exhilarated laughter soon followed between panting breaths.

"Do...you think...they saw us?" Betty wheezed; hands braced on her knees.

Elizabeth shook her head, equally winded. "Too dark...but we...got what we...needed." She patted her camera triumphantly.

Their chuckles subsided as the gravity of their find sank in. The proof was damning - Bailey's truck with the driver-side tires coated in mud. At Worthington Station she remembered seeing one side of tire tracks in the mud and then the other side in gravel. This was enough evidence to cast doubt on poor Hobo Jeff's guilt.

Sobering, they walked slower now, replaying each detail to ensure they missed nothing. The chill night air cooled their flushed cheeks. Elizabeth glimpsed Samuel's profile in the moonlight, strong and handsome. A powerful rush of affection washed over her unexpectedly. He took Elizabeth's hand without thinking to guide them further into the woods.

The narrow path was canopied by branches and flooded with silvery light. Elizabeth should have dropped Samuel's hand, but instead held tighter, remembering far different nighttime wooded wanderings from years ago.

They slowed further until stopping entirely, all three hushed and alert to the symphony of sounds around them. The relaxing sound of the Olentangy River in the distance. Leaves rustling in the gentle wind with a shivering, silken sound.

Elizabeth's eyes had adjusted to the veiled light. She could just make out the contours of Samuel's face as he gazed at her intently. He seemed about to speak when a violent rustling broke the spell.

All three whirled towards the noise as branches thrashed violently ahead on the path. A large figure was lumbering straight towards them with an orange glow visible, still obscured by vegetation. Samuel and Betty froze.

Years of quick thinking with her students kicked in for Elizabeth. Without hesitating, she scooped up a large fallen branch and hurled it with all her might toward the approaching creature.

A resonant thud followed by a strange yelp confirmed she had hit her mark. Elizabeth leaped up with her camera in her hands and took the last two photos on the camera film with the flash of lightning striking! The unknown person or beast crashed off in the opposite direction, cracking branches growing fainter until they faded away completely.

Elizabeth laughed in a release of nervous energy while Betty whistled appreciatively. "Lizzie's still got that pitcher's arm! What on earth was that thing?" Samuel just shook his head in wonderment at her instinctive act of courage.

Their amusement was short-lived, however. A heavy limb snapped, echoing behind them - the person was circling back! Wasting no time, Samuel yelled "This way, hurry!" pulling Elizabeth off the path into the dense trees.

Thorns tore at their clothes and hair as they plunged recklessly into the blackness. Betty's labored wheezing revealed she was close behind. Low-hanging branches whipped Elizabeth's face, but she pressed on, Samuel's hand firm around her hands.

At last, the trees thinned ahead, opening to a moonlit field. The meadow's long grasses tangled their feet, but they ran on, no sounds of pursuit behind them now. They ran across Granville Road towards the high school and closer to Elizabeth's house.

As their adrenaline ebbed, Betty voiced the question they all pondered. "But what in heaven's name was that? A person or wild beast?" neither could provide an answer.

They assessed themselves for injuries - only minor cuts and scrapes, plus Betty's broken wristwatch. Eventually catching their breath, the chase seemed more and more surreal. Had it been an elaborate prank?

Too weary to ponder further, they continued through into the village. Nearly safe, they began to relax, till a strange glow ahead almost sent them ducking behind bushes. But it was only the moon rising over Worthington's water tower.

Betty determinedly led the way before breaking the tense silence. "Let's not fret or make wild guesses. We'll take this slowly and scientifically. Elizabeth, you'll need to get those photos developed and analyzed."

Samuel and Elizabeth nodded, comforted by her rationality. But chills still rippled through Elizabeth picturing the hulking silhouette that had barreled towards them. What had they stumbled into?

Elizabeth paused, struck by the idyllic fall moon's beauty. Seeing her gaze, Samuel dared to take her hand again. "No monsters here," he murmured.

Elizabeth managed a smile, feeling the truth in his words. A return of hope punctured the fear and doubt that had shrouded her for so long. Whatever unknowns lay ahead on their quest, she knew with certainty she did not walk alone. With Samuel, Betty, and even dear Aunt Gracie's spirit beside her, the light would prevail.

Chapter 7: Trick or Fright

When Thursday morning came, Elizabeth wanted nothing more than to hide under the covers. But duty called, so she rose to dress herself and prepare breakfast. Even oatmeal and tea could not revive her mental acuity.

The surrealness of the previous night seemed now like a strange dream in the mundane light of day. Had there been a hulking creature under those moon-bathed trees? Or were the shadows just playing tricks?

Her camera film would confirm or disprove their eerie encounter. On instinct, Elizabeth grabbed the necklace Aunt Gracie had gifted her, seeking clarity and courage for the day ahead.

Outside, late October's vibrant hues were slowly fading and scattered on the frosty ground. Halloween would come tomorrow and the little ghosts and goblins would be begging for candy, signaling a step closer to winter. The seasons never paused their endless cycle, unaware of Worthington's struggles. Elizabeth quickened her pace, ready to battle the forces of chaos and darkness.

At school, she maintained a brave face, leading the children in recitations and arithmetic drills. But her mind wandered to graver matters. She kept replaying the scene in the woods the previous night: Was someone dangerous right here in their midst?

During the lunch recess, Elizabeth slipped away to the high school. As she walked in, she heard the sounds of the cadence of typewriters.

She glanced in and saw the young women practicing their typing skills. Elizabeth smiled recalling her typing class not too long ago.

"Miss Russo!" exclaimed a young man's voice. It was Danny, the high school senior who snapped the photo with her class on the Village Green recently and the time she nearly got hit by the Model T. She knew Danny when he attended the Worthington School and remembered him fondly.

"What are you doing here?" he asked.

"I was hoping that someone could help me develop my camera film. I'm kind of working on a mystery." said Elizabeth.

"Well, Miss Russo, I'm just the guy to help you. Let's go to the darkroom."

Danny guided Elizabeth into the high school photography darkroom, the smell of chemicals strong in the air. He turned off the regular lights and switched on the lights that had an eerie red glow. With practiced hands, he removed the film from her camera and began the development process - immersing it in different baths as images slowly emerged on the negatives. Elizabeth watched anxiously, eager to see the evidence from the night's investigation.

As the photos continued developing, the first images that appeared were bittersweet reminders of the past. Elizabeth with her beloved father at the Ohio State Fair. She saw their smiling faces enjoying ice cream cones outside the dairy barn just weeks before he passed away. As Danny hung the photos to dry, the memories brought a swell of emotion and nostalgia, making Elizabeth wistful for simpler times with her father. Danny saw her reaction and gave her a compassionate pat on the back.

"Is that your father?" Danny asked.

"Yes, he was a wonderful man and I miss him very much." sighed Elizabeth.

"I'm sure he would be proud of you, Miss Russo!" Danny replied.

Allowing her a quiet moment with the ghosts of the past, Danny continued to process the film, watching new clues to develop before their eyes.

She saw the photos of the muddy tire prints she took just outside Worthington Station by Hobo Jeff's shack. Then, the photos she took at Milkman Bailey's place the night before. She could see Kelsey Hayes written on the rims and Goodyear 18" x 3 5/8" on the tire. She quickly wrote down the details in her notebook.

Elizabeth grabbed the photos.

"Thank you, Danny. I appreciate this," said Elizabeth.

"Anything for you, Miss Russo," said Danny, blushing.

Elizabeth then hurried back to the elementary school. She was anxious for the school day to end so she could follow up on this new evidence. Finally, the last bell rang and the students rushed out.

Elizabeth met Betty waiting on the Village Green. She eagerly showed Betty the photos Danny had developed. Betty held up the shots of the mud tracks and the photos taken at Bailey's house, scrutinizing them closely.

"Remarkable, these are a match to Milkman Bailey's tires from last night! This is solid proof of his truck being at the crime scene," Betty said.

She shook her head in amazement at their breakthrough. The photo of the strange glowing eye in the woods was unfortunately too blurry to make out any details.

"We need to send these to Goodyear to see if they match," replied Elizabeth.

The two women crossed High Street and walked over to the Worthington Library on the northeast side of the Village Green. Inside they found Mary Joe, a librarian, Elizabeth had known growing up from school.

"Mary Joe, can you look up the mailing address for Goodyear tires please?" asked Elizabeth.

"Certainly, Elizabeth, let me grab the Akron, Ohio, phone book."

Mary Joe came back and opened up the phone book and flipped through the pages.

"Here you go Elizabeth. This is the address for Goodyear Headquarters." Mary Joe pointed to the address with her index finger.

Elizabeth quickly wrote the address down in her notepad.

"Thank you, Mary Joe," said Elizabeth.

"No problem. I hope you find what you are looking for."

While waiting, Elizabeth took out a pen and paper, drafting a letter asking Goodyear if the tire tracks photographed in the mud were consistent with the Goodyear 18" x 3 5/8" tire treads found on Milkman Bailey's truck. If so, are these types of tires common on other types of vehicles? She placed the photos and letter into an envelope.

"Ok, Betty, let's walk over to the Worthington Post Office to get this letter mailed," Elizabeth said.

"Sounds like a plan," Betty replied with a grin.

As Elizabeth and Betty walked out of the library, the Worthington News on the counter caught their eye. The front-page headline read, "Milkman Bailey of Gabel Dairy Found Dead!"

Elizabeth and Betty gasped and grabbed the paper. According to the article, Milkman Bailey's body had been discovered inside his house. Police suspected he tripped down his stairs and hit his head during the night. When he didn't show up for work the next day, one of the employees went to his house and saw his body lying on the floor.

"This is unbelievable," Elizabeth muttered as they scanned the story. "First Mr. Collins, now Milkman Bailey. It's like we're living in a nightmare."

Betty shook her head grimly. "And after we were just at Bailey's place investigating. This is no coincidence. Someone is trying to cover their tracks."

Elizabeth nodded, rolling up the chilling newspaper article. Darkness was encroaching, but she refused to let evil prevail.

With the Goodyear envelope in hand, they headed to the post office to mail the letter. As they walked south on the Village Green Elizabeth shivered, feeling suddenly exposed out on the quiet street. The safe predictability of life in Worthington now seemed fractured beyond repair. What sinister forces were at play in their once peaceful village?

As the two approached the Worthington Savings Bank, they looked up at the looming water tower that stood behind the bank.

"At least the water tower is looking over us." chimed Betty.

The two stopped at the Red and White to buy Halloween candy for the following evening. Inside, John was working behind the counter. He greeted them warmly.

"Good evening, Elizabeth!" said John, smiling. "How was your day?"

"Informational," replied Elizabeth, holding the letter.

Elizabeth and Betty grabbed some Hershey's chocolate bars, ribbon candy, and candy corn to hand out for Halloween.

"If only I found my Jello recipe, I could give that out to the children," said Betty smiling.

"Gotta keep those kiddos happy and hopped up on sugar!" John joked as he rang up the sweets.

"Oh, can you also throw in some stamps for my envelope please, John?" Elizabeth asked.

"Not a problem, Elizabeth," he replied.

Elizabeth managed a polite smile despite her churning thoughts about last night's death. She didn't want to alarm John or spread rumors, so she stayed mum about the troubling headlines.

After paying and placing the stamps on the envelope, Elizabeth and Betty continued to the post office down the street. Elizabeth dropped her letter in the outgoing mailbox, hoping for swift answers from Goodyear.

Clutching the paper sack of treats, she bid Betty good evening to head home to prepare for the classroom Halloween party that was to be held for the children the following day. But inwardly, her mind raced with questions about who was behind the deaths shadowing Worthington.

Once Elizabeth was home, the telephone rang. It was George, whom she hadn't spoken with in days after his rude behavior at Aunt Gracie's funeral.

"Elizabeth, I must apologize again for my boorish actions," George said contritely over the line. "Seeing you with Samuel, I allowed old jealousies to get the better of me. Can you forgive me?"

Elizabeth hesitated, but George did sound genuinely remorseful. "I accept your apology," she replied. "This has been a difficult time for us all."

"Quite right, my dear. Please, allow me to make it up to you over dinner Thursday evening. There is a new restaurant that just opened in North Columbus." George offered.

Despite her lingering hurt, Elizabeth acquiesced, hoping they could reconcile and move forward. "Alright, dinner Thursday then."

They exchanged stilted goodbyes before hanging up. Elizabeth sat pensively for a moment, doubts resurfacing about their compatibility. But she resolved to give George another chance and try enjoying a pleasant evening together.

For now, distracting herself with Halloween preparations was a welcome relief from both relationship woes and the pall cast over Worthington. She focused on preparing decorations for the classroom and organizing games, determined to bring some lightness back to her students during the dark times.

Elizabeth tried lying down to rest, but the incessant ticking of the clock kept her mind racing. Restless, she decided to head up to the New England Inn for a nightcap.

She walked into the dim, smoky barroom and glanced around. A big band song on the radio was playing. Sitting at the bar was Dr. Bentley, cigar in hand, chatting up Jane from the Lady Alice Beauty Salon. Elizabeth slid onto a stool a few seats down from them.

"Let me guess, Elizabeth, the Coca-Cola High Ball?" grinned Jimmy, the bartender with a confident look. "You know me," Elizabeth replied with a wry smile.

As Jimmy poured her drink, Elizabeth's gaze drifted back to Dr. Bentley. The glowing ember of his cigar disconcerted her. Just then she reminisced on the strange glowing eye she'd seen in the woods. Could that be what I saw last night, she thought.

Compelled to investigate further, Elizabeth grabbed her drink and subtly shifted seats to get a better vantage on Bentley and Jane's conversation. Through the haze of smoke, she strained to overhear their discussion.

"Bailey had it coming, no one liked him anyways" Bentley was saying quietly. Jane looked anxious. "People said he had a gambling problem," Jane said.

Elizabeth's pulse quickened, though she couldn't hear enough context to grasp their full meaning. Were they connected to the recent deaths?

Just then, Bentley glanced up and noticed Elizabeth watching them. He abruptly tossed some bills on the counter and stood.

"Best be going. Pleasure talking with you, Jane," he said tersely before brushing past Elizabeth and about to exit the door.

Elizabeth sat stunned, more convinced than ever of Bentley's involvement in the shadows engulfing Worthington. She had to act fast. As Bentley turned to leave, Elizabeth hurried over and bumped into him.

"Oh, I beg your pardon!" she exclaimed.

Bentley glared at her angrily. "You! You're that woman from the cemetery. You need to mind your own business and stop being so inquisitive about the Collins family affairs."

Elizabeth stood her ground. "Maybe you shouldn't be so concerned with making little Amy a Hollywood movie star."

Bentley's face turned red. "How dare you!" he spat. "I'm an old friend of the family trying to help them in their time of mourning. It's disrespectful of you to imply otherwise."

He tried to push past Elizabeth but she sidestepped to block him. "It's all rather suspicious if you ask me. What exactly is your interest in the Collins family, Dr. Bentley?"

His eyes flashed dangerously. "My interests are none of your concern. Now, get out of my way before you regret it."

He roughly shoved past her and stormed out the door. Jimmy and the other patrons were all staring at the confrontation. As Bentley hurried out, Elizabeth's gaze fell on the cigar he was holding. Through the haze of smoke, she could just make out the label - "LaProsa."

She filed this detail away, knowing the cigar information could be a useful clue. The ornate label and quality tobacco weren't commonly found around Worthington.

Elizabeth finished her drink quickly, mind racing. She left a tip for Jimmy and made her way home, replaying the tense confrontation.

As Elizabeth walked home, she gazed up at the moon, which had an eerie blood-red hue tonight bright enough to illuminate the entire town.

She shivered thinking about Milkman Bailey's shocking death. Reading the newspaper article, police claimed that he had merely tripped down some stairs and fatally hit his head on a vase. But the timing after their encounter, especially with the men arguing, seemed too coincidental.

Passing by her own house, Elizabeth was struck by a notion. She changed direction, heading for Milkman Bailey's residence instead.

Perhaps under the light of this ominous blood moon, some new clue would be revealed.

The milkman's home was dark and still when she arrived. Elizabeth hesitated, then stealthily made her way to the side of the house. She strained for any illumination in the windows, ears pricked for the slightest sound.

Rounding to the back entrance, she stifled a gasp. The door hung crookedly ajar, swaying in the cold autumn breeze. Someone had been here since the police investigation.

Heart pounding, Elizabeth peeked inside the darkened kitchen. "Hello?" she called softly. No response except the creak of the broken door.

The blood moon cast everything in an eerie crimson glow, but she could discern no movement within. Still, Elizabeth couldn't shake the sense she was being watched from the shadows.

Fear mounting, Elizabeth turned to leave the milkman's house. But on impulse, she decided to return to the woods where they'd seen the mysterious glowing eye the other night.

She walked into the darkened forest, shivering as the wind stirred the leaves. Elizabeth made her way to the area where she, Betty, and Samuel had hidden from the ominous figure.

Pausing in a moonlit clearing, Elizabeth took a deep breath to steady her nerves. The red moon cast light between the trees. "It's okay," she whispered to herself.

Scanning the ground, something small caught her eye. She bent down and picked it up, examining it in the crimson light. It was a battered, ashy cigar. Turning it over, she could just make out the label, "LaProsa."

Elizabeth's pulse quickened. This had to be one of Dr. Bentley's cigars! It must have fallen when he was lurking here the other night. She hastily pocketed the evidence.

Nearly giddy with excitement, Elizabeth hurried out of the woods. This felt like a breakthrough. She needed to tell Betty about finding Bentley's cigar immediately.

Elizabeth rushed to Betty's house and breathlessly knocked on her door. Betty answered in her nightgown and was half awake. Elizabeth related the discovery. Betty's eyes widened as she examined the exotic cigar.

"Well, I'll be! This is finally the proof we need of Bentley's connection," Betty exclaimed. She patted Elizabeth's hand proudly. "You've cracked this case wide open, Gumshoe! Now we just need to force his hand into a confession."

Elizabeth grinned, adrenaline and hope surging through her veins. The twisted puzzle pieces were at last coming together to expose evil's plan. Light would prevail over darkness - she was certain of it now.

The next day at school, Elizabeth's students were abuzz with excitement about trick-or-treating that evening. She had the children bob for apples and let them enjoy some of the candy she'd purchased earlier.

Little Amy Collins came up to Elizabeth, practically bouncing with enthusiasm. "I'm going to dress up as Dorothy from The Wizard of Oz tonight!" she exclaimed. "Sometimes I like to play Wizard of Oz by the river in the woods. I have the dress, the ruby red shoes, and everything!"

Elizabeth smiled at her delight. Soon the final bell rang and the kids rushed out, ready for candy and costumes.

As Elizabeth walked home, she felt a sense of peace and confidence that progress was being made in solving the mystery. Finding Bentley's cigar felt like a major step towards justice.

The crisp autumn air carried the happy shouts of children gathering jack-o-lanterns and preparing for tonight's festivities.

As evening fell, Elizabeth turned on her porch light and arranged the treats. Soon, adorable trick-or-treaters began arriving fairies, pirates, ghosts, and, of course, little Amy as Dorothy.

Placing candy in each outstretched bag, Elizabeth found comfort in this quaint tradition. No matter how dark and chaotic the world was, the laughter of Worthington's children kept hope alive.

It was late and Elizabeth had finished handing out candy. She blew out the candle in her pumpkin on the porch and then headed inside.

She spent some time on the couch and read over the notes she and Samuel had written in her notebook. Her eyes started to drift and Elizabeth knew it was time to go to bed. As she walked down the darkened hall towards her bedroom, a loud thud made her jump. Who would come calling this late, she wondered anxiously.

Elizabeth hurried to the front door and swung it open, gasping at the sight. Her jack-o-lantern was smashed to pieces on her front door and had fallen onto the porch. Among the pulpy mess, she spotted a scrap of paper.

Hands shaking, she picked it up and read the chilling message scrawled in jagged letters: "You'll love lying in Walnut Grove!"

Elizabeth recoiled in terror. Walnut Grove was where Aunt Gracie had just been buried. Was this a threat to her life?

Frantically, she slammed the door and locked it. Then she shoved a kitchen chair under the knob. Heart pounding wildly, she peered out the window but saw only darkness.

Someone knew she was digging around and wanted her silent. Elizabeth considered going to the police, but Officer Jameson had brushed off her theories so far. She thought of Samuel and Betty, but no, she couldn't endanger them too.

Elizabeth paced anxiously, feeling utterly alone and hunted. The evil plaguing Worthington had her directly in its sights now. She had stumbled onto something far more twisted than she realized.

But she refused to cower or back down. If they wanted her in Walnut Grove Cemetery, they'd have to put her there themselves. Elizabeth would stand and fight whatever darkness was converging - even if she had to do it alone.

Chapter 8: Rumble at the Game

Elizabeth barely slept, unnerved by the chilling threat left on her doorstep. As daylight crept in, she mulled over who would do such a thing. Was it Dr. Bentley? The ominous note proved she was getting closer to unraveling this mystery, and that made someone desperate.

Mustering her courage as the morning brightened, Elizabeth carefully picked up the piece of paper and went to show Betty. Her hands trembled, but she refused to be paralyzed by fear.

Elizabeth knocked urgently on Betty's door; the chilling note clenched tightly in her fist. Betty emerged in her nightgown, blinking awake.

"What is it, dear?" she asked worriedly, seeing Elizabeth's distraught state.

Elizabeth burst into tears, holding up the piece of paper. Betty quickly ushered her inside and settled her on the couch. "I'll put some tea on," she said before heading to the kitchen.

Elizabeth continued weeping as the kettle boiled. Betty returned with steaming mugs of Earl Grey and a plate of her famous lemon bars.

As they sipped their tea, Elizabeth described the pumpkin smashing and ominous message left outside her home. "I was too shocked and afraid to come get you last night. I'm sorry," she finished tearfully.

Betty patted her hand reassuringly. "There, there, don't you worry. From now on you come straight here whenever you need to. We're partners in this investigation, after all."

She drew Elizabeth into a comforting embrace. "With everything that's happened - losing Gracie, your mother not coming back. This was the last straw."

Drawing back, Betty's expression hardened with determination. "But we are going to the police station right now about these threats. I'm calling a cab."

At the station, Officer Jameson had Elizabeth come into his room and had Betty wait in the hallway. Elizabeth urgently recounted everything: the pumpkin threat, seeing Bailey's truck near the crime scene, the eerie glowing eye in the woods, and their suspicion of Dr. Bentley's involvement.

"I know Hobo Jeff is being framed," Elizabeth insisted. "The real killer is still out there."

Officer Jameson took out his notepad, holding up a hand. "Now, Miss Russo, I know your intentions are good, but we have a confession from Jeff for Mr. Collins' murder. He gave it to us just before the Franklin County Sheriff's Office took him into custody."

He continued gently, "As for Mr. Bailey's death, he was a known drunkard who likely stumbled down those stairs. And that 'beast' you saw was probably just some teens smoking in the woods. LaProsa cigars are made right here in Ohio and all sorts of people smoke them, not just Dr. Bently."

Jameson put a hand on her shoulder. "Take it from me, Dr. Bentley is a good man and a good friend of the Collins family. He was away at a conference in Chicago when Collins was killed. I know that because we're in the same poker club. He was away that week."

Elizabeth was crestfallen. "But officer, I swear something sinister is happening in Worthington!" Jameson just smiled sympathetically. Elizabeth pressed Jameson about the voices at Bailey's house and the pumpkin threat, but he dismissed it all as misunderstandings and pranks.

As she left his office, Jameson pulled Elizabeth aside while Betty waited in the hall. "Okay, okay. We'll increase the patrols around your street. Now look Miss Russo, I know you mean well, but please leave this to the professionals," he said sternly. "Focus on teaching, not amateur sleuthing."

He leaned in and whispered, "And frankly, it's not good for you to spend so much time with Betty. She has a history of wild imaginings. We've been called about her ranting before. Don't get sucked into her eccentric conspiracy theories."

Elizabeth bristled but held her tongue. Storming out, she found Betty waiting expectantly.

"That man is impossible!" Elizabeth fumed. "He all but called me a hysterical woman caught up in fantasy. I know what I witnessed, Betty!"

Betty nodded firmly. "Of course, you do. And we're not giving up, no sir! Investigating is in my bones, so don't you listen to that condescending policeman."

Elizabeth felt heartened by her stalwart friend. "You're right. We're the only ones trying to shed light on the darkness plaguing this village. We'll keep pursuing the truth, no matter what Jameson thinks."

Linking arms, the two women marched out of the station, heads held high. Elizabeth was through being dismissed and intimidated. With Betty by her side, she would unravel this mystery, no matter how sinister the forces aligned against them. The light of truth would prevail.

The following week passed tensely but uneventfully. True to their word, police presence increased substantially, keeping the shadow forces temporarily at bay.

Fall deepened, and leaves transformed Worthington into a dazzling palette of gold, orange, and red. With Halloween past, thoughts turned to November and the upcoming fall harvest festival held annually uptown that weekend.

The approach of the festival brought comfort to Elizabeth, signaling life and renewal continued even amidst the lingering darkness. Worthington's heart still beat resiliently if uncertainly.

Elizabeth taught her students the history of the festival and its spirit of gratitude. Their innocent excitement lifted her spirits. She volunteered for decoration duty at the festival, determined to spread some light.

As Elizabeth walked into downtown Worthington, she looked up and still noticed the village's water tower painted with "Beat Groveport!" she smiled, reminded of the long-standing tradition for Worthington High students to sneak up and graffiti the tower with slogans against their big football rivals, the Groveport Cruisers. But she also shuttered at the thought of a student accidentally falling from the tower. Some merchants had also put up signs in their windows saying "Squash Those Cruisers!" and "Cardinals Soar Above!"

Thursday evening arrived, and Elizabeth dressed up for her dinner date with George, determined to enjoy a pleasant night out of town.

George arrived in his father's sleek black sedan, honking the horn gallantly. Elizabeth emerged in a simple black dress, managing a smile.

"I thought we'd try that new place, the Blue Danube," George said as they drove down High Street towards Columbus.

Inside the restaurant, the host welcomed them to the restaurant. "Or as we like to call it, the Dube!" he proclaimed with a flourish, leading the two to a candle-lit table and handing them menus. A slow ballad was being played on the radio and Elizabeth needed the calmness for a change.

After ordering wine, George reached across the table for Elizabeth's hand. "I do apologize for being so pushy about the wedding lately. Work's just been a bear preparing for year-end."

He smiled gently in the candlelight. "But how have you been holding up, sweetheart?"

Elizabeth considered unloading all her suspicions about the murders. But the wine was so relaxing, and the restaurant's muted bustle soothing. She decided to simply enjoy an evening's reprieve from the chaos.

"Oh, just keeping busy with school and staying out of trouble," she replied lightly. Their food arrived aromatically steaming.

"Garlic baked chicken for the lady and beef stroganoff for the gentleman." said the waiter as he placed the steaming plates on the table.

As they ate and chatted about innocuous topics like work and books, the knotted tension inside Elizabeth slowly began unwinding. She let the wine and George's familiar presence set her mind temporarily at ease.

By dessert, a warm haziness had settled over her with her slice of apple pie. For the first time in weeks, the shadows encroaching on Worthington felt held at bay. Not solved permanently, but kept safely in the periphery for an evening.

After dinner, George dropped Elizabeth off at home kissing her in the car. The two walked up to the front porch. He gestured to the markings left on the door from the smashed pumpkin.

"What happened here?" he asked with concern.

Elizabeth tensed slightly, not wanting to worry him. "Oh, probably just some mischief-making high schoolers," she said lightly. "You know how they are on Halloween."

George's eyes narrowed briefly but then he seemed to accept this. "Well, let me know if you have any more trouble. I'd be happy to patrol the neighborhood to keep an eye out."

"That's very kind of you," Elizabeth replied. "But I'm sure it was just a harmless prank."

She said goodnight and gave him another kiss before George could inquire further. Inside, she leaned against the closed door with a sigh. The evening had been a nice distraction, but she couldn't keep brushing off George's questions forever. Nor could she avoid facing the threats encircling her.

Looking around the darkened and empty house, Elizabeth shivered. She thought of calling Samuel or Betty for comfort but decided not to disturb their evenings.

Tomorrow she would resume her investigation with renewed determination. But for now, she double-checked the locks and retreated to her room. Lying in bed with the covers pulled tight, she stayed alert to any suspicious sounds in the creaking old home.

Exhausted yet vigilant, Elizabeth finally drifted off, the necklace from Aunt Gracie clutched in her hand. She found some solace knowing she did not stand alone against the shadows looming over Worthington.

The next morning dawned bright for a beautiful fall Friday. Elizabeth awoke feeling well-rested for the first time in weeks. She brewed some coffee and ate a bowl of Kellogg's Pep cereal.

Stepping outside, she was greeted by the sight of Betty in her nightgown waving excitedly. "Good morning! Hey, don't forget the football game tonight. It's the Worthington Cardinals versus the Groveport Cruisers. The Cards haven't won a game all season. We should go cheer them on!"

Elizabeth hesitated. "Oh, I was thinking I'd just relax at home tonight."

But Betty waved her hands impatiently. "Nonsense! It'll be good for you to get out and socialize. Come on now, what do you say?"

Looking at her neighbor's eager face, Elizabeth relented with a chuckle. "Alright Betty, you win. I could use a fun outing. But I can't stay too late, I have the fall harvest festival preparations tomorrow."

"Atta girl!" Betty cheered. "We'll have a grand time. Nothing like a game night in the village!" She hurried back inside to get ready.

Elizabeth had to admit she was looking forward to the normalcy of the evening. The familiar chants and cheers would help overpower the echoes of fear and tragedy that had pervaded Worthington.

That night, bundled against the autumn chill, Elizabeth and Betty strolled over to Worthington High amongst other chatting neighbors. The crisp air rang out with school spirit. For a few hours at least, the pall would lift.

The school spirit was contagious. Arriving at the field, they bought hot chocolates from the concession stand and joined in cheering raucously for the Cardinals with the rest of the crowd.

Cheerleaders on the sidelines hollered encouragement as the teams charged out. Elizabeth felt swept up in the boisterous atmosphere. During exciting plays, Betty whooped and hollered right alongside the teenage fans.

Before they knew it, Worthington was up 14-7. One family loudly rang out a dinner bell that echoed downfield amongst the excitement. Laughing and clapping along to the cheers, Elizabeth was enjoying the game.

The cheerleaders energetically rallied the crowd all game long. They performed backflips and pyramids, never letting the energy lag.

Whenever the Cardinals scored or got a first down, the cheerleaders would erupt in choreographed dances, pompoms waving as they jumped and kicked in unison.

Their infectious enthusiasm had the packed bleachers on their feet chanting "Go, Cards, Go!" the cheer captain winked and blew kisses to the crowd.

Near the goalpost, the Cardinals cardinal mascot was playfully mocking the lumbering Cruiser horse mascot.

When the Cruisers failed to score on fourth down, the Cardinal gleefully did laps around the dejected horse much to the crowd's amusement.

The Worthington marching band also put on spirited performances before and during the game. They paraded near the field blaring out the fight song on trumpets and pounding the drums.

During tense moments in the game, the band would strike up rousing tunes to rally the team and crowd. Their thundering beats and soaring melodies electrified the atmosphere. At halftime, the band began to march onto the field for their performance.

As the band started playing, Elizabeth and Betty decided to stretch their legs and get more hot chocolate. As they waited in the concession line, a familiar voice called out "Elizabeth."

She turned to see Samuel waving and walking over with his uncle. "Fancy running into you ladies here," Samuel said with a grin.

"Betty, this is my Uncle Howard," introducing the white-haired man. "He was my ride over for the game. Uncle Howard, you've already met the amazing Elizabeth Russo and this is her neighbor Betty."

"A pleasure to meet you, Betty, and it's great to see you again amazing Elizabeth," Replied Howard smiling politely, while shaking their hands. "Any friends of Samuel's are friends of mine."

"So, are you ladies enjoying the game?" Samuel asked.

Betty nodded eagerly. "Oh yes, we're having a marvelous time! It's been too long since I've been to a good football game."

"Well, we're glad to see Worthington giving those dreadful Cruisers a walloping. It's about time we start winning a game!" Howard chuckled. "Makes me feel years younger! I'd best get back to my seat but wonderful to meet you ladies."

He tipped his hat and headed off. Samuel smiled warmly at Elizabeth, his brown eyes twinkling. "I'm really glad you came tonight. This is just what we all needed."

Elizabeth agreed, warmed by the friendly chance encounter. As Elizabeth chatted with Samuel, an irate voice suddenly interrupted. "What are you doing with him?!"

She turned to see a fuming George marching towards them, eyes blazing. The smell of alcohol wafted off of him.

"I warned you to stay away from this rascal!" George shouted, getting right in Samuel's face.

Before anyone could react, George pulled back and took a wild swing at Samuel. As George's fist flew the Worthington marching band started to play, "Night on Bald Mountain" which was recently popularized in the *Fantasia* movie. Elizabeth and Betty cried out, but Samuel managed to dodge the blow.

"Whoa there fella, calm down," Samuel said evenly, hands raised. "No need for trouble here."

But George was nearly in rage. "Don't tell me to calm down!" The brass on the football field built up the tension in the song as they kept marching the field. George took another sloppy swing that Samuel evaded. "I'll teach you to mess with my girl!" People were starting to stare at the confrontation.

One high schooler yelled, "Give him the old brass in the face knuckle sandwich!"

Betty tried intervening but George shoved her back. As George took another drunken swing, this time his fist connected with Samuel's face, striking him in the cheek.

Samuel staggered back, clutching his face as Uncle Howard looked on in shock. Before anyone could react, Samuel scowled and clenched his fist, swinging back and landing a solid punch to George's face.

"Why you little..." George snarled as the sound of the brass horns swelled. He tackled Samuel to the ground and the two men began brawling fiercely right there on the sidelines.

Fists flew and grunts rang out as they wrestled and exchanged blows. Danny came running in with his camera in hand and started taking snapshots. Elizabeth and Betty shrieked for them to stop but the men were lost in a drunken rage.

The crowd backed away as the fight rolled into the ground. George managed to pin Samuel down and got in a few more hits before Samuel kneed him in the stomach. The band had now stopped to see what all the commotion was about.

Wheezing, George loosened his grip allowing Samuel to flip him over. Now Samuel was on top, ready to punch George's face.

Just then police officers came charging over to break it up. They pulled the bloodied men apart and dragged them off each other. They took hold of George's arms. "Okay pal, I think you've had enough fun for tonight," Officer Jameson said sternly. "Let's go sleep it off."

George cursed and struggled but they dragged him off towards the exit. Elizabeth stood shaking, horrified at his actions. Samuel scuffed up with a bloody nose, put a comforting hand on her shoulder.

"I'm so sorry about that," Elizabeth said softly. "We'd best get home before any more trouble arises."

As the police escorted George away, Samuel's Uncle Howard hurried towards them looking baffled.

"What in blazes was that all about?" he exclaimed.

Samuel wiped the trickle of blood from his busted lip and shrugged. "Oh, you know, just a minor disagreement between gentlemen," he joked weakly.

But Elizabeth was too upset to find any humor in it. "That was appalling behavior, from both of you!" she scolded.

Samuel at least had the decency to look ashamed under her glare. "You're right, I'm sorry," he said sincerely. "George just has a way of bringing out the worst in me. But I shouldn't have taken his bait."

Howard put a hand on his shoulder. "Come on now, let's get you cleaned up at home. Miss Russo is displeased by your roughness."

As Samuel stood with his uncle, Elizabeth just shook her head in disappointment. She expected better from him than such brute violence, no matter the provocation.

Betty linked her arm supportively. "Men! Brawn over brains every time, if you ask me," she clucked disapprovingly. "Don't fret dear, this too shall pass."

As Samuel turned to leave with Howard, his uncle suddenly stopped and faced the ladies again.

"You know ladies, it's just a few weeks but, we'd be delighted if you two joined us for Thanksgiving dinner," Howard proposed warmly. "The more the merrier!"

Elizabeth opened her mouth to decline, still miffed at Samuel, but Betty jumped in enthusiastically. "We'd be honored! Wouldn't we, Elizabeth?"

She gave Elizabeth a pointed look. Recalling her mother was away in Cincinnati, Elizabeth reluctantly agreed. "Alright, dinner would be lovely, thank you."

"Excellent!" Howard beamed. "We're happy to welcome friends at our table. I'll leave you two to make amends," he added with a wink at Samuel.

With their Thanksgiving plans unexpectedly set, Elizabeth and Betty said goodnight. Samuel gave her a conciliatory smile and wave as he departed with his uncle.

Betty took Elizabeth's arm cheerfully. "There now, doesn't a holiday feast sound nice?"

Elizabeth just sighed, hoping the dinner would not add further fuel to existing tensions. But Betty's gift of forcing cheer into gloom was hard to resist. Between the cheerleaders' boundless pep, the dueling mascots' antics, and Samuel and George's fistfight, Worthington High displayed a bold team spirit against their rival. But Elizabeth felt she had too much excitement for the night and decided it was time to leave the football game early. After the halftime fiasco, Betty and Elizabeth walked back to their houses respectfully under the watchful glow of the harvest moonlight.

Chapter 9: The Fall Harvest Festival

The next day, Elizabeth awoke early to an unusually warm November morning. Fetching the Worthington newspaper, "The Newspaper that puts service before dollars" the main headline read, "Cards Win First Game, Beating the Groveport Cruisers." Underneath the headline was a photo that Danny had taken of Samuel and George fighting the night before with the headline reading, "Halftime Brawl Interrupts Football Game". Elizabeth shook her head in disgust.

Just then, the roar of a motorcycle approached. It was George, sporting a fresh black eye. Even before dismounting, he began shouting accusations of Elizabeth "two-timing."

"You're a two-timer, Elizabeth Russo! I knew you were up to no good with that Samuel Lewis!" he said drunkenly.

Elizabeth opened the door and shouted.

"I've done no such thing!" she insisted, but George remained belligerent.

"Look, George," Elizabeth said, holding up the newspaper. "You've made the front page. Are you happy now?"

"Get some sense into yourself, Elizabeth!" yelled George.

"I have and I have finally had enough!" said Elizabeth as she slowly removed the engagement ring from her finger.

"It's over, George," she said with finality, dropping the ring into his hand. "I tried to make this work but I can't take the jealousy anymore."

Just then Betty emerged in her nightgown. "What's all this hootin' and hollerin so early?" she scolded.

"Get back inside, you old hag!" George spat venomously.

Betty planted her fists on her hips. "Let me fetch my rolling pin so I can give you another shiner!"

With a sneer, George with the ring in hand, peeled off down the street on his motorcycle, leaving a trail of smoke.

Elizabeth felt surprisingly calm, a weight lifted from her shoulders. She had reclaimed power over her own life. Betty squeezed her hand supportively.

Elizabeth proclaimed, "He's such an ass!"

"Holy cow, you just learned that!" replied Betty.

"You know Elizabeth, you're the type of woman that's not easily controlled."

"Thank you, Betty, it took me a long time to figure that out!' winked Elizabeth.

Gathering her things for the Fall Harvest Festival uptown, Elizabeth steeled herself to face the gossip and whispers about the fight the night before and her broken engagement that were sure to follow. But she refused to feel embarrassed or ashamed. Elizabeth and Betty headed uptown to help decorate for the festival. Elizabeth wanted to focus her energy on something positive for the community.

In downtown Worthington, other volunteers were busy transforming the space into an autumn wonderland. People were stringing up colorful leaves, carving jack-o-lanterns, and arranging bouquets of wheat, sunflowers, and gourds.

Elizabeth got to work hanging paper maple leaves around the concert stage and painting signs with fall motifs. The repetitive tasks soothed her frayed nerves after the dramatic confrontation with George that morning.

"These leaves are just lovely, Elizabeth," Betty remarked approvingly. "Your artistic talent is shining through!"

Praise from the usually particular Betty buoyed Elizabeth's spirits. She found satisfaction in creating something beautiful for her hometown, especially during such dark times. The cheery downtown was a testament to Worthington's resilience.

She was reminded that her light came from within, regardless of any man or any situation. And today, she would continue shining it brightly at the fall harvest festival alongside friends and neighbors. The coming of winter could not diminish the warmth of their communal bonds.

Soon High Street was closed down for the festivities. A lively crowd gathered, embracing the warmth of fall in the air.

Children laughed and played games like apple bobbing. Elizabeth smiled watching them and almost got roped by a boy dressed as the Lone Ranger attempting to lasso her for fun.

"Whoa there, partner!" she said, playing along while neatly sidestepping his rope. The boy grinned with his toy pistol and ran off to find more targets.

Elizabeth wandered among rows of arts and crafts booths displaying their wares: wood carvings, quilts, homemade jams, and baked goods. The scents of cinnamon and apple cider wafted through the fall air.

On the main stage, the singer said the title of the next song is called, "Fall Harvest Hoedown." The lively bluegrass band started playing an upbeat, foot-stomping number. The standup bass plucked out a thumping rhythm while a wiry musician scratched rhythmically on the washboard.

Elizabeth tapped her toes along to the driving mountain music as she browsed the booths. It reminded her that just a county or two away lay the start of the Appalachian hills and the rich culture there.

The banjo player picked out a twangy solo, his fingers flying over the strings. The fiddler began enthusiastically sawing away, fedora tilted rakishly as he played.

The music pulsed with heart and history, transporting listeners to Appalachian hollers and front porches. Even city slickers like teacher Miss Greener could be spotted trying to learn the steps as dancers whirled by them whooping.

Watching her neighbors revel in the homespun melodies, Elizabeth felt connected to generations past who had found joy in humble traditions. The timeless music was the thread bonding the community. Swaying along, Elizabeth clapped her hands.

Seeing Worthington residents reveling together under the morning sunshine, spirits seemed lifted from the gloom of recent events. Wandering through the festival, Elizabeth noticed little Amy Collins competing in the corn husking contest. She gave the girl an encouraging smile, but Amy's mother shot Elizabeth an icy glare that hurried her along.

Farther down the street, Elizabeth glimpsed Samuel leaning against the balcony of the New England Inn, tapping his foot to the music drifting up. His nose was bruised from last night's scuffle.

Elizabeth approached hesitantly. "How are you feeling?" she asked, indicating his injury.

Samuel gave a rueful chuckle. "I've felt better, but I'll live." His expression turned serious. "Elizabeth, I'm deeply sorry for letting my temper get the better of me. I hope you can forgive me."

Seeing his sincerity, her lingering frustration melted away. "Of course, Samuel. Let's put it behind us."

He visibly relaxed. "I'm relieved to hear that." Glancing around at the merrymaking, he added "This is a great festival, bringing folks together."

Elizabeth followed his gaze to the smiling faces surrounding them - kids with candy apples, couples dancing, friends chatting over cider.

Samuel smiled firmly and offered his arm as the band struck up another rousing mountain reel. Together, they stood on the steps of the Inn. Elizabeth put her arms around Samuel's waist. As they embraced,

Elizabeth was struck by how comforted and protected she felt in Samuel's arms. She drew back to look up at him seriously.

"I broke off my engagement with George," she confessed.

Samuel's eyes widened in surprise. "I hope it wasn't only because of the fight on my account."

Elizabeth shook her head. "It wasn't just last night. Many issues have been compounding." She took a shaky breath. "The truth is, my heart is being pulled in another direction."

At this, Samuel tensed slightly. "What do you mean?" he asked guardedly.

Elizabeth squeezed his hands, summoning her courage. "I mean towards you, Samuel. You're my guy. I've never stopped caring for you. Being with you these past weeks, I feel like I've come home."

Samuel stood speechless for a moment before a smile spread across his face. "Oh, Elizabeth...I feel the same way. I never should have left you all those years ago."

He gently cradled her face. "If you will still have me, I want to make things right between us."

Elizabeth's eyes brimmed with happy tears. "There's nothing I want more."

As Samuel leaned in tenderly, the festival swirled around them like leaves in the wind. But Elizabeth was lost in the feeling of his lips against hers - a kiss that tasted of new beginnings.

Elizabeth's heart pounded as Samuel drew back from the tender kiss. She felt as though a huge weight had been lifted now that her true feelings were out in the open.

Giving his hands an affectionate squeeze, she said "I need to leave here for a bit. There's someone I need to visit."

Samuel looked curious. "Oh? Who's that?"

"Hobo Jeff," Elizabeth replied. "He's innocent in all this and I mean to prove it. I'm going to try talking to him again to see if he remembers anything more about that night."

Samuel nodded understandingly. "That's a fine idea. Let me walk you home."

Elizabeth smiled, gratitude welling up at having such a supportive partner at last. Arm in arm, they made their way through the festive crowd.

As Elizabeth and Samuel approached her house, they spotted postal carrier Mr. McFoley placing letters in her mailbox.

"Afternoon Miss Russo!" he called out cheerfully. "Got an envelope here for you, looks like it's from the Goodyear company."

"Thank you, Mr. McFoley!" Elizabeth said, hurrying over to take the letter while Samuel lingered behind her.

Seeing the Goodyear logo, her pulse quickened. This must be a response to her inquiry about whether the tires she took photos of were used on any specific vehicles.

Elizabeth tore open the envelope eagerly and unfolded the letter. It read:

"Dear Miss Russo,

Thank you for contacting Goodyear regarding our Kelsey Hayes 18" x 3 5/8" tires. That particular model is standard issue for use on all milk delivery trucks manufactured by Ford. The tire track patterns you photographed in the mud and the tire treads on the tire without mud do appear to match. Please let us know if you need any other information.

Sincerely,
John Dorsey
Goodyear Tire Company"

Elizabeth could barely contain her excitement as she showed Samuel the letter. "This proves the tire tracks outside Hobo Jeff's belong to Milkman Bailey's delivery truck!" she exclaimed. "It's concrete evidence against him."

"What good is it if he's dead?" replied Samuel.

"Well, at least we know he's involved in planting the knife." said Elizabeth.

Clutching the letter, Elizabeth hurried along filled with hope and vindication. The darkness was receding at last.

Elizabeth felt emboldened by Samuel's steady presence. She would help exonerate poor Jeff, expose the real killer, and banish the darkness from Worthington once and for all.

As Samuel bid Elizabeth farewell, she picked up her phone and called for a cab. She requested a ride to the state penitentiary where Hobo Jeff was being held. She had scheduled a meeting with him at 2 P.M. that afternoon.

As the cab pulled up, the temperature took a deep dive. Before walking outside, Elizabeth grabbed her coat and placed the letter from Goodyear in her coat pocket. As the cab driver took her to downtown Columbus, gray clouds started to burst with rain.

"Well, it is Ohio in the fall," Elizabeth said to the driver as he pulled up to the prison.

After checking in at the front desk, she was escorted to the visiting room. Soon, Jeff appeared in his black and white striped uniform, shuffle-stepping in leg irons. Elizabeth was taken aback by his transformed appearance. His formerly scraggly hair and beard were neatly trimmed.

"Jeff, it's so good to see you," Elizabeth said warmly as he sat down across from her. "You're looking well."

Jeff nodded. "I reckon being locked up forced me to clean up some. Haven't touched a drop of liquor since getting hauled in here."

He leaned forward eagerly. "Finding it real hard convincing folks I'm innocent though. You're the only kind soul who believes me, Miss Russo. I sure appreciate you coming."

Elizabeth patted his hand reassuringly. "I know you didn't kill Mr. Collins, Jeff. I'm going to keep investigating until your name is cleared, I promise."

Elizabeth hesitated, then said carefully, "Jeff, Officer Jameson told me that you confessed to killing Mr. Collins after I first spoke with you. Is that true?"

Jeff looked down shamefully. "Yes ma'am, I did confess, but only because that policeman tricked me into it."

He went on bitterly. "Jameson said that if I just admitted to the crime, I wouldn't get a death sentence. But I ain't guilty! I was just scared of dying on the chair, so I told him what he wanted to hear."

Jeff met her eyes pleadingly. "You've gotta believe me, Miss Russo, I never laid a hand on Mr. Collins. But that policeman kept pressuring me to own up to it. I didn't know what else to do."

Elizabeth was appalled but unsurprised at Jameson's underhanded tactics. She grasped Jeff's hand firmly. "I do believe you. Officer Jameson took advantage of your vulnerability. But we're going to make this right, I promise."

Jeff wiped his eyes, overcome with gratitude. Elizabeth's resolve to expose the truth hardened. She refused to let the innocent suffer to protect the guilty.

"I have my trial next month, just before Christmas." Jeff continued gloomily. "They tell me I'll likely get life in prison." Overwhelmed, he dropped his head into his hands and began weeping.

Elizabeth immediately moved to comfort him, gently patting his back. "There, there, we're going to clear your name before then. I promise."

She leaned into the distraught man. "Have faith. You are innocent and we're going to prove it."

Just then, a stern guard appeared. "Alright, time's up."

Jeff dabbed his eyes as he was led away in shackles. "Bless you, Miss Russo." he called over his shoulder.

Elizabeth sat quietly gathering her emotions before departing the stark prison. She was now in a race against time to exonerate Jeff before his sentencing. Failure was not an option - she refused to let him pay for another's sins.

With truth and justice on her side, she would bring the real killer to light and restore freedom to the gentle-hearted vagrant. The shadows could not withstand the brilliant beacon of truth for long.

As Elizabeth was exiting the prison, the guard called for her to come with him. She was led into a dimly lit room.

Inside, a man in a suit and a hat sat at a desk smoking a cigarette. "Miss Russo? I'm Detective Morris with the Franklin County Sheriff's Homicide Unit," he introduced himself.

"I wanted a quick word since I'm the lead investigator on the Collins murder case." Leaning forward intently, he asked, "Do you have any information that could aid our investigation?"

Heart pounding, Elizabeth rapidly relayed everything - her certainty of Hobo Jeff's innocence, the evidence against Milkman Bailey, the mysterious cigar, and Officer Jameson's unwillingness to pursue other leads.

Detective Morris scribbled notes, nodding along. "I see...this is quite illuminating. Do you know of any motives on why someone would want Mr. Collins dead?"

Elizabeth wrung her head nervously. "Possibly Dr. Bently was having an affair with Mrs. Collins, but I have no proof. Maybe Milkman Bailey had a beef with the Collins family. I don't know. So, what should I do?"

The detective leaned back on his chair. "You just keep on your path, Miss, and let me worry about law enforcement's role. Discretion is of the utmost importance here."

Though somewhat cryptic, his assured tone heartened Elizabeth. Help was coming; she just needed to stay the course towards the truth.

Thanking the detective profusely, she hurried out, feeling emboldened. Shadows were slowly receding as mysteries came to light. Worthington's fate hung in the balance.

Just before leaving, Elizabeth quickly mentioned the Goodyear letter confirming the milk truck tire treads, as well as her photographic evidence.

"Do you have those photos and letters?" Detective Morris asked.

"Yes, I can give those to you," Elizabeth said, pulling out the letter from her coat pocket and handing it to Detective Morris.

"Here is the letter from Goodyear. It was Danny, a senior from Worthington High School, who helped me develop the photos. I don't have them here." replied Elizabeth. "I can give those to you later. Can I contact you with any further information?" she asked urgently.

"Don't worry, I'll reach out to you discreetly if needed. For now, please just carry on as usual." He gestured for her to close the door.

Still bursting with questions, Elizabeth reluctantly left the detective's office. The cab driver was waiting outside to take her back home.

"Back home, ma'am?" he asked her.

"Yes, back to Worthington, please," Elizabeth replied, settling into the seat. She watched the grim prison fade into the distance as the sun started to make its way through an opening in the clouds. Hope and trepidation churned within her.

The detective's interest seemed promising, but the urgency was building. Time was running short for poor Jeff facing sentencing. And whoever killed Mr. Collins and Milkman Bailey were surely desperate to keep their secrets buried.

Staring out at the passing farmland, Elizabeth steeled her nerves. She was in too deep to turn back now. Cloaked in shadows, the remorseless killer may still be lurking. But she would illuminate the darkness, no matter the risk. Justice would prevail.

As the cab rattled up the country road, Elizabeth mulled over Detective Morris' question: What motive was behind Mr. Collins' murder? She realized investigating that angle further could be key to cracking the case wide open. And that likely meant returning to the scene of the crime for clues.

Elizabeth's pulse quickened at the thought of going back to that house, but it had to be done. Perhaps examining Collins' study or personal effects would provide insight into why someone wanted him dead.

She considered who might have access to let her look around. Little Amy was too young, and Mrs. Collins seemed to resent Elizabeth's snooping thus far. That left Dr. Bentley, "the friend of the family" who Elizabeth still suspected of shady involvement. But appealing to his ego as a concerned citizen might persuade him.

Arriving home, Elizabeth hurried to the phone and rang the doctor's office not knowing if he would answer on a Saturday. She took a steadying breath as his gruff voice answered the phone.

"Hello?" he asked.

"Dr. Bentley? This is Elizabeth Russo. I wonder if we could discuss something privately regarding the Collins case?"

There was a weighty pause. Finally, Bentley replied "Come to my office first thing tomorrow morning. Don't be late." The line clicked dead.

Elizabeth shuddered slightly. It felt like making a deal with the devil. But she reminded herself that solving a murder meant getting one's hands dirty. First thing tomorrow, she was going to look evil straight in the eye.

Chapter 10: The Winds of Change

The next morning, Elizabeth dressed simply and headed to Dr. Bentley's office to meet with him, feeling equal parts dread and determination.

Upon arrival, she was shown back immediately to an examination room. The space was cramped and chilly, with various anatomical diagrams on the walls that gave Elizabeth a chill.

After a few minutes, Dr. Bentley entered clasping a manila folder. "Nosy girl, aren't you?" he said gruffly by way of greeting.

Elizabeth stood her ground. "I'm just a concerned citizen seeking the truth."

Bentley seemed to appraise her shrewdly. Finally, he spoke, "If you must go on amateur sleuthing, Mrs. Collins needs help boxing up Frank's study. I suppose I could arrange a supervised visit."

Elizabeth's spirits lifted, but she replied evenly "That would be quite helpful, thank you."

"Come along then. And not a word of this, or your 'visit' ends immediately," he commanded. Elizabeth simply nodded.

They drove in tense silence to the Collins home. Its windows were now dark and cheerless. Inside, Amy sat playing listlessly while her mother sorted papers.

While Dr. Bentley hovered ominously, Elizabeth searched the study for any telling clues about Frank Collins' life or death. The hours passed tensely but uneventfully as she quietly combed through documents while placing them into boxes.

Just as they were finishing, Elizabeth spotted a framed photograph of Collins and Bentley, smiling together with a prized hunting trophy. Her blood ran cold.

Afterward, Bentley warned her again to stop meddling or face consequences. But the image stayed seared in Elizabeth's mind. What were those two men tangled up in? She was getting closer to finding the true killer. She could feel it.

As mid-November descended on Worthington, the brilliant orange and tan leaves were finally relinquishing their grip on the trees. Elizabeth kept busy raking up the windblown piles from her front yard, only to have them scattered again by wind gusts.

Betty came outside to check on her, bundled against the chill. "My goodness, it seems you're fighting a losing battle with these blustery winds," she called out.

Elizabeth, smiled ruefully, brushing flyaway leaves from her red scarf. "It's a never-ending task, but it keeps me occupied."

Seeing her friend's weariness, Betty squeezed her shoulder. "It's been a hard season, but better times are coming. Keep your spirits up."

With Betty's help, they finally wrangled the leaves into some semblance of order. Elizabeth stood back surveying their work, leaves racing past her feet again.

"You're right Betty, I can't control the winds," she mused. "But I can brace myself and do my best until they pass."

Betty nodded.

Arm in arm, they went inside Betty's house for hot cider by the fire. Elizabeth felt warmed, knowing she didn't have to weather storms alone. With steadfast friends and faith, she would make it through the blustery seasons unfalteringly.

As they sipped cider, Betty was bustling about, muttering "Now where did I put that Jell-O recipe? I simply must find it before the holidays!"

As the sun went down, Elizabeth gazed into the flames, a photo on the mantel caught her eye - Betty's late husband, Harold. Betty followed her glance and chuckled.

"Ah yes, my dear Harold. I suppose I should introduce you properly." She lifted an ornate urn on the fireplace mantel that was next to the photo. "Harold's ashes are in here. Someday I hope to have a ceremony spreading his ashes at the fishing creek in England where he fished as a boy."

Elizabeth blinked in surprise but tried not to show it. "What a... lovely tribute to Harold," she managed.

Betty beamed. "He was a wonderful man - kind, patient, always game for adventures." She dabbed her eyes. "I suppose that's why I'm still trying to solve mysteries even at my age. Keeps that spirit of adventure alive."

"I never got to know Harold," said Elizabeth. "I was just always busy with life and school. I wish I would have taken the time to know him better. Matter of fact, before this whole tragedy, I really didn't know you either."

"There, there, that's just how life goes sometimes. Everyone is in a rush to do this or that. Tragedies can bring people together and that's what it did for the two of us." Betty replied.

Seeing Betty's indomitable spark despite the loss, Elizabeth felt humbled. If her friend could face darkness with courage and cheer, so could she. They would navigate the storms together.

"Speaking of mysteries, I've been mulling over potential motives behind the Collins murder," Elizabeth said. "But I'm stumped on any solid theories."

Betty set down her tea decisively. "Well, it's never too late to search for more clues!"

Seeing Elizabeth's hesitance, she waved a hand. "Oh poppycock, it's not that late! Why don't we head over to the Collins' house tonight and have a discreet poke around?"

"I don't know Betty...Besides, I was just over there today and didn't find anything," Elizabeth hesitated.

But Betty was already fetching her coat and hat. "Come now, it's already dark. Grab your camera and notepad. No time like the present!"

Unable to curb her neighbor's enthusiasm, Elizabeth reluctantly got her things. Put some new film in her father's old camera and met Betty outside. They then hurried down the quiet street to the Collins' home.

"We'll just take a quick sweep of the premises and be on our way," Betty whispered conspiratorially.

The house was still and gloomy in the encroaching dusk. Elizabeth's pulse quickened as they peered into dark windows, looking for signs of life.

Approaching the driveway at the side of the Collins darkened home, Elizabeth and Betty crept up to their trash can, hoping for clues. Removing the lid, Elizabeth peered inside the empty bin.

Betty shone her flashlight along the interior of the can. "Aha, there's a piece of paper stuck to the side!" she exclaimed.

Just then, a noise sounded from the backyard. Startled, Elizabeth hastily grabbed the paper and tucked it in her pocket.

She and Betty dove behind a nearby bush just as a porch light flicked on. Crouching low, they watched a shadowy figure emerge to investigate, heartbeats thundering.

After what felt like an eternity, the door closed again and the house went dark. The women remained huddled in tense silence for several more minutes just to be sure.

Finally, Betty whispered, "I think the coast is clear." Carefully they emerged from the bushes.

Elizabeth's hand shook slightly as she uncrumpled the discarded document retrieved from the trash. In the dim light, they made out what looked like a torn check memo.

"Do you think this could be important evidence?" Betty asked in a hushed voice. Elizabeth nodded firmly. "I'm going to find out. One way or another, I'm getting to the bottom of this mystery."

Clutching the paper like a lifeline, she knew the risks now mattered little. She would unravel the sinister secrets that had plagued Worthington, no matter what dangers lay in wait.

A light suddenly switched on in an upstairs window. Muffled voices that were arguing drifted out from the open pane.

Betty grabbed Elizabeth's arm excitedly. "Quickly, let's get closer to eavesdrop!"

They snuck around to the backyard where a large tree stood close to the illuminated window. "Climb up and see if you can overhear who's arguing," Betty urged.

Elizabeth hesitated. "That tree is too high. I could never climb it."

But Betty was undeterred. "Nonsense, I'll give you a boost up. Now, put your foot on my hands and I'll lift you to that lower branch."

"But Betty, I don't want you to get hurt," Elizabeth protested.

Betty scoffed "Hurt? I may be 60 years young but I'm spry as a spring chick! Now hop up, we're losing time."

Reluctantly, Elizabeth allowed Betty to hoist her up into the tree's lower boughs. Heart pounding, she slowly scaled higher while Betty kept watch below.

Reaching a sturdy branch near the window, Elizabeth steadied herself and listened intently to the quarreling voices inside. She could just make out a man and a woman...

Peering through the window, Elizabeth could scarcely believe her eyes. There stood a scantily clad Mrs. Collins wearing some sort of red lace bustier with Dr. Bentley shirtless before her.

"Well, aren't they the happy new couple," Elizabeth whispered to herself wryly. She shifted higher in the tree, trying to catch their heated argument.

"I'm telling you, it's too risky to try anything further now," Bentley was saying in an agitated tone.

Mrs. Collins crossed her arms angrily. "You said you'd handle this! How long must we keep living in fear?"

Bentley gripped her shoulders. "Just be patient a little longer. I've worked too hard to let it all unravel now."

Elizabeth strained to hear more, but they moved away from the window. She had heard enough. They were conspiring about something sinister.

Crouched precariously on the tree branch, Elizabeth strained to hear more of the argument through the open window.

"This is all your fault!" Mrs. Collins shrieked, jabbing her finger at Dr. Bentley. "We could've been lounging on a California beach if your plan with that blasted milkman hadn't fallen apart!"

Bentley took a swig from a bottle of scotch. "Well excuse me, but it's not my fault the insurance company is dragging their feet on your husband's $50,000 life insurance payout!"

Elizabeth's eyes widened. $50,000 life insurance policy? That certainly sounded like a motive for murder. She hurriedly scribbled notes in the moonlight as the tree branch wobbled under her.

Just then a strong gust whipped up, nearly blowing Elizabeth out of the tree. She clutched the trunk tightly, heart lurching as the unfinished note fluttered away into the blackness below.

From inside came the sound of breaking glass and renewed shouting. "This is a mess; you need to fix it, Edgar!" Mrs. Collins cried shrilly.

Edgar...so that was Dr. Bentley's first name, Elizabeth realized. More useful information. She committed as much as she could to memory.

The wind subsided, allowing Elizabeth to quickly whisper while hanging on the branch, the bombshell details to Betty cautiously waiting below.

"This proves it's all about money," she whispered. Betty's eyes gleamed. "We've got them now! We must go to Detective Morris immediately."

Elizabeth nodded firmly. The pieces were falling into place. Come morning light, their shadowy scheme would be exposed at last.

Elizabeth listened intently as Dr. Bentley tried reassuring Mrs. Collins.

"Don't worry, you'll get the insurance money soon, and I'll collect on my poker winnings from Jameson," he told her. "As long as he owes me gambling money, I can keep him in line."

Just then, the sound of a child crying came from the other room. "Ugh, why is that girl still up? I already put Amy to bed." Mrs. Collins scowled.

As she stormed off, Elizabeth realized this might be her only chance to photograph them together. She steadied her camera just as a gust of wind whipped up.

The flash bulb popped brightly, illuminating the yard. Startled, Elizabeth lost her balance and tumbled out of the tree with a thud.

"Oof!" she grunted as she hit the ground. Betty rushed over and urgently helped her up. Just then, they heard Mrs. Collins bellow "Who's out there?!"

Adrenaline surging, the women sprinted away just as the porch light flicked on. They didn't stop running until safely back at Betty's house, hearts pounding wildly.

"Do...you think...he saw us?" Elizabeth gasped.

Betty shook her head. "I don't believe so. But that was a close one!" She turned to Elizabeth excitedly. "Tell me, did you get the photograph?"

Gingerly, Elizabeth pulled out the camera. "I think so," she said. Elizabeth and Betty hurried home. Elizabeth placed the camera on the kitchen table and hoped to develop the film soon.

The next morning at school, Elizabeth noticed little Amy Collins' desk was empty. She stepped into the hall to ask the principal if he'd heard from Mrs. Collins about Amy's absence.

"No, she hasn't called in today," he said, looking concerned.

An hour later during lessons, the principal knocked urgently and said Mrs. Collins was on the phone insisting to speak with Elizabeth right away.

Elizabeth rushed to the office phone, pulse racing. "Mrs. Collins? Is everything okay?" she asked anxiously.

"It's Amy, she's gone!" Mrs. Collins cried hysterically. "She wasn't in her room this morning. I've looked everywhere!"

Elizabeth gripped the phone tightly. "Stay calm, I'll be right there," she said in her most soothing teacher's voice.

"Principal Gentry, can you please cover my classroom? Amy Collins has gone missing!" Elizabeth breathlessly asked.

"Of course, Elizabeth," he replied.

She grabbed her coat and purse. The principal called after her, "Keep me informed!" She rushed out the door without a word, focused on reaching the Collins' home.

Had something awful happened to Amy? Was she hurt, or worse? Elizabeth refused to assume the worst yet. Amy adored school. She wouldn't just run off, unless she was scared.

Elizabeth picked up pace, praying they would find the little girl safe. She thought of the confrontation last night. Had Amy heard something sinister? Swallowing hard, Elizabeth hurried on.

When Elizabeth arrived at the Collins' house, a distraught Mrs. Collins confronted her angrily. "Did you tell Amy to go somewhere?" she demanded. "That girl seems to listen to you!"

Elizabeth held up her hands. "No, I haven't spoken to her. I have no idea where she could be."

Mrs. Collins just slammed the door in her face. Elizabeth searched the neighborhood streets for any sign of Amy but found nothing. Growing more worried by the minute, she went to see if Betty had noticed anything odd.

Betty was on her porch, waving. "Home for a quick lunch, dear?"

"No Betty, Amy Collins is missing!" Elizabeth cried breathlessly. "She never showed up at school today."

Betty gripped Elizabeth's arm, face paling. "Good Lord. Poor child, who knows what trouble she could run into alone."

Thinking fast, Betty grabbed a coat. "You keep canvassing the neighborhood. I'll gather up a search party. We'll scour every inch of Worthington if we must!"

Elizabeth felt a rush of gratitude for Betty taking charge. With her friend's help, surely, they'd soon locate the vulnerable girl unharmed. She refused to consider any darker alternative.

They must find Amy before someone with sinister intent does. Elizabeth recalled the heated argument Amy might have overheard last night. What secrets had the girl unearthed? Shaking off dread, Elizabeth hurried on in pursuit of answers.

After finding no trace of Amy in the neighborhood, Elizabeth headed home to fetch her father's camera in case they needed evidence. But approaching her back door, she gasped. The glass was shattered and the door was left ajar!

Signaling frantically to Betty, they cautiously entered the house. Elizabeth saw that her camera was missing from the kitchen table where she'd left it.

Venturing further inside, drawers were flung open, and clothes were strewn around her ransacked bedroom. Elizabeth's heart sank realizing she'd been robbed.

"Oh dear, what a violation," Betty murmured, surveying the mess. "Though it does suggest you're on the right track uncovering the truth."

Elizabeth nodded grimly. She was certain this was retaliation for spying last night. But personal threats mattered little now. Finding Amy was all that concerned her.

"The camera will have to wait. We must keep searching for that child," she said resolutely, grabbing her coat and relocking the damaged door.

Betty gave her hand a supportive squeeze. "You're right. With luck, others have picked up the search by now."

Hurrying downtown, Elizabeth saw with relief that was true. A small group of neighbors combed the streets calling Amy's name. She would not rest until the girl was safe.

The hunt stretched on as the short autumn day darkened. But Elizabeth refused to give up hope. They would light the way through Worthington's shadows and bring Amy home.

Chapter 11: The Policy of Truth

As dusk fell with no sign of Amy, Elizabeth's mind raced to think of clues to the girl's whereabouts. Suddenly, she remembered something Amy had mentioned after trying on her Halloween costume.

"Sometimes I like to play Wizard of Oz by the river in the woods," the girl had happily once said.

Outside of their houses, Elizabeth gasped and turned to Betty. "I think I know where she might be. The Olentangy River! Grab your flashlight!" Betty nodded excitedly. "Will do. Let's hurry!"

Elizabeth rushed into her house where she quickly phoned Samuel, catching him up in a rush. Soon he pulled up in his uncle's car.

"Get in, we're going to the river!" Elizabeth cried. Samuel stepped on the gas as they sped off.

Samuel drove the car west passing the high school on Granville Road. He then pulled off the road. The three walked towards the river. Drawing closer, Betty scanned the darkened woods with her flashlight. "There, by that big oak tree. Stop!" Elizabeth exclaimed.

Peering into the gloom, she spotted a small figure in a blue dress. The figure's arms wrapped around a tree with the Olentangy River's water raging around it. Heart leaping, Elizabeth jumped out and ran over. "Amy!"

"Miss Russo!" cried, Amy.

Amy looked up, frightened but unharmed. There was just enough patch of land below to prevent her from being swallowed by the river.

"I'll get the rope from the car!" Samuel said.

Soon he was back with rope in tow. He tied a loop around the rope like a lasso. Just like a cowboy wrangler, Samuel threw the rope to Little Amy.

Motioning to put the rope loop around her waist, Amy grabbed it.

"Tie it around your waist, sweetheart!" yelled Samuel.

"What if you let go of it?" questioned Amy fearfully.

"I won't sweetheart. Tie it tight!" Samuel said with confidence.

Amy managed to get the rope around her waist just as the river's raging water knocked her off the patch of land.

With all their effort, Elizabeth and Samuel pulled the little girl to shore with Betty shining her flashlight the entire way.

Samuel scooped the little girl up in his arms. Removing the rope, Amy was wet and coughing, but okay.

Elizabeth swept her into a tight embrace. "You're safe now, sweetie, it's okay."

With Samuel carrying Amy back to the car and wrapping her up in a nice warm blanket, she met Elizabeth and Betty's relieved smiles. The search was over, ending in joy. Darkness had not prevailed that night.

In the car, Elizabeth gently asked Amy, "Why did you come out here, sweetie?"

Amy sniffed back her wet tears. "Mom and Dr. Bentley were fighting something awful last night. I thought maybe the Wizard of Oz lived in these woods and maybe he could make things okay again."

Elizabeth stroked her hair soothingly. "It's all right now, you're safe." She tucked the blanket around the shivering child.

They soon arrived at Amy's house. When she emerged tired but unharmed, Mrs. Collins came flying out the door.

"Where have you been? You could've froze to death!" she cried, grabbing Amy's shoulders.

"I'm sorry, Mama," Amy mumbled, head down. Mrs. Collins just clutched her daughter tight, relief washing over her features.

Samuel squeezed Elizabeth's hand before driving off. Watching Amy reunite with her mother, Elizabeth was filled with gratitude. The long night had ended well for the little girl.

She bid them goodnight and walked wearily home with Betty. Though questions remained, at least innocence had prevailed tonight. The storm clouds were dissipating over Worthington.

Returning home, Elizabeth was crestfallen to find all the evidence she'd gathered - the cigar, Goodyear letter, photos - had been stolen in the break-in. She felt hopeless about making progress now.

Just as she was about to break down in tears, Elizabeth felt something in her pocket. Pulling it out, she realized it was the small notebook she used to scribble case notes. Flipping it open, the paper scrap from the Collins' trash fell out.

Picking it up, Elizabeth examined the document closely. It was a voided check made out to Jacob Bailey for $500 for "services rendered", and signed by Dr. Edgar Bentley.

Elizabeth's eyes widened. This must be payment to Milkman Bailey for his role in their twisted scheme. A vital piece of evidence after all!

New determination coursed through Elizabeth. The break-in had been a desperate, foolish move by the culprits. They didn't realize she still held this damning clue.

Running next door, Elizabeth burst into Betty's and breathlessly filled her in. Betty's eyes gleamed. "Well now, they're not as clever as they thought!" She patted Elizabeth's hand. "This is the beginning of the end!"

Elizabeth nodded firmly, clutching the precious scrap. The light of truth was proving impossible to extinguish.

As November progressed, the day arrived for Elizabeth and Betty's Thanksgiving dinner invitation at Samuel's Uncle Howard's house. They dressed nicely and took a cab over.

"Oh, confound it, I'm still hunting for that Jell-O recipe to make my famous dessert," Betty tutted.

When they arrived, Samuel, Uncle Howard, and Howard's wife, Rosemary, welcomed the two. Betty insisted on helping Rosemary prepare the stuffing. But she became distracted chatting and let it burn to a crisp in the oven.

Chaos ensued with smoke billowing through the kitchen as Howard and Betty frantically tried airing out the mess.

"Good heavens, Betty, you've incinerated it!" Howard exclaimed in dismay.

"Oh, fiddlesticks! Clearly, I'm no domestic goddess," Betty admitted sheepishly.

Elizabeth tried not to laugh at the debacle. Samuel gave her a playful wink. "Not to worry, we'll scrape together a feast yet," he assured Howard.

Despite the rocky start, they were able to cobble together a delicious turkey dinner with all the fixings. Preparing the hearty meal, spirits were merry and warm. Elizabeth gazed happily at her make-shift family, feeling profoundly grateful.

During a private moment, Samuel asked Elizabeth how her investigation was progressing. She dejectedly shared that a lot of her evidence had been stolen during the break-in.

"I'm feeling ready to give up," she admitted. But Samuel embraced her reassuringly.

"Don't lose heart," he urged. "You're so close to cracking this case wide open."

Bolstered by his encouragement, Elizabeth resolved to keep pursuing the truth. Soon they gathered in the dining room with Howard, Rosemary and Betty for the feast.

The table practically groaned under the spread of food - a golden roasted turkey, savory sage dressing, sweet potato casserole, green bean casserole topped with crunchy fried onions, fluffy biscuits with homemade jam, and plenty of cranberry sauce and gravy.

As they passed plates around the dining room table, Betty turned to Samuel. "So, how is your insurance business apprenticeship coming along with your uncle?"

"Quite well," Samuel replied after swallowing a mouthful of turkey and gravy. "Learning the ropes on life insurance policies and claims has been fascinating."

He gave Elizabeth a meaningful look. She realized this expertise could be useful in unraveling Mr. Collins's life insurance policy mystery. New possibilities glimmered in her mind.

The meal passed enjoyably, full of warmth, laughter and good company. Despite lingering shadows over Worthington, this gathering kindled light. Elizabeth cherished it, gaining strength for the fight ahead.

During a lull in the conversation, Betty remarked "You know, I really should update my life insurance policy, Howard. What sort of coverage did Mr. Collins have?"

Howard wiped his mouth delicately. "Well Betty, I can't divulge specifics about another client's policy. But I'd be happy to assess your needs and find a suitable plan."

Betty clasped her hands eagerly. "That would be swell! Elizabeth, dear, you're off school tomorrow. Why don't you join me so we can see Samuel in action at the office?"

"I'd be delighted," Elizabeth replied, catching Samuel's eye across the table. This could be the perfect chance to gain insight into Collins' mysterious policy.

"Excellent, come by tomorrow morning and we'll take good care of you," Howard declared.

Elizabeth smiled but inside felt a twinge of guilt about somewhat duping Howard. But revealing the full truth was still too risky. For now, gaining a deeper understanding of the life insurance policy could prove key.

After dinner, Howard's wife cleared the dining room table, for tea and dessert. But Samuel took Elizabeth's hand first and drew her aside to the fireplace in the living room. A romantic melody was playing softly on the radio.

Samuel pulled Elizabeth close and began slowly swaying to the music. As they danced, he gazed at her tenderly.

"When I left Worthington all those years ago, I didn't know if I'd ever see you again," he murmured. "Having this second chance with you now...it means everything."

Elizabeth's heart swelled and she rested her head on his shoulder. "I feel the same way," she whispered. "Like fate brought us back together."

She closed her eyes contentedly as they continued revolving in front of the flickering fireplace. The outside world slipped away, and it was just the two of them connected once more.

After a blissful interlude, Samuel tilted her chin up and kissed her softly yet passionately. Elizabeth melted into the embrace, the rest of the room falling away.

As they lingered by the fireplace, the radio program turned to the story of how FDR this year officially moved Thanksgiving back a week, making it the third Thursday of November instead of the fourth. He hoped this would help stimulate the economy with the longer Christmas shopping season.

"In the spirit of gratitude, I'm giving thanks for you this year, Elizabeth," Samuel said tenderly, pulling her close.

Elizabeth's cheeks flushed happily. "And I'm so thankful to have you back in my life, Samuel."

He smiled and brushed his thumb against her cheek. On the radio, FDR's voice rang out proudly proclaiming Thanksgiving as a day to celebrate community and blessings.

Elizabeth gazed up at Samuel, reflecting on how much she cherished this unexpected gift of a second chance together. Despite all Worthington's troubles, this time with him was the light guiding her through the darkness.

Samuel leaned in for one more soft kiss before they joined the others. Hand in hand, they walked into the dining room, hearts overflowing with love and gratitude. Bellies full and spirits lifted, they soon bid their hosts goodnight. Back home, new energy coursed through Elizabeth. The shadows had not defeated her yet. With Samuel lighting the way, she would uncover the truth and see justice done, no matter the obstacles.

The next morning, Elizabeth and Betty arrived at Howard's insurance office. His wife, Rosemary, who also worked as Howard's secretary, welcomed the two. While Rosemary spoke with Howard in the back room, Betty slyly handed Elizabeth a small camera.

"I'll keep Howard occupied. You sneak to the back and photograph Mr. Collins' policy file," she whispered conspiratorially.

Betty then strode up to Howard, peppering him loudly with questions about life insurance rates and coverage options. As they became engrossed in conversation, Elizabeth slipped unnoticed down the hall.

Her pulse pounded as she quickly scanned the file room labels. Finding a drawer marked "Clients C-D", she slid it open and rifled through until she located Frank Collins' folder.

Hands trembling, she flipped it open and hastily snapped photos documenting the $50,000 policy and listed Mrs. Collins as the primary beneficiary.

As Elizabeth was crouched over sneakily photographing the Collins file, she suddenly heard footsteps approaching down the hall. She froze, heart lurching.

A moment later, Samuel appeared in the doorway, stopping short when he saw her.

"Elizabeth? What are you doing back here?" he asked.

Panicked, she quickly stammered "Oh! I was just, um, looking for the ladies' room and got turned around." She slipped the camera into her pocket discreetly.

Samuel raised an eyebrow. "I see. Well, the washroom is at the front, not the file room."

He studied her face closely. Elizabeth tried to look innocent.

Finally, Samuel said gently "I won't ask any more questions. But be careful, okay?" He turned to leave then looked back. "I trust you have a good reason for any risks you're taking."

Elizabeth's shoulders relaxed in relief. "Thank you, Samuel. And I do, I promise."

He nodded before heading out. Elizabeth exhaled shakily, grateful for his faith in her despite the suspicious circumstance. She hurried to finish and join Betty, evidence now secured. Elizabeth crept back up front just as Betty was wrapping up.

As Elizabeth rejoined them, Betty told Howard, "Well, you've given me a lot to think about on policy options. I'll mull it over and be in touch."

"Excellent, let me know if any other questions arise," Howard replied jovially, shaking their hands.

Betty and Elizabeth bid Samuel and his uncle goodbye for now. Outside the office, Betty turned to her eagerly. "Well, were you successful?"

Elizabeth smiled and discreetly showed her the camera. "Got everything we need."

"Marvelous!" Betty exclaimed. She linked her arm through Elizabeth's as they strolled away. "Now we're getting somewhere. I knew we'd make a fine sleuthing team."

Elizabeth laughed, spirits lifted. With the incriminating evidence secured, the end was in sight. The darkness that had plagued Worthington was no match for two determined women seeking justice.

Chapter 12: The Christmas Crystal Ball

December had arrived in Worthington, with cold air and flurries portending snowier days ahead. As Christmas break neared, Elizabeth's students grew restless with holiday excitement. She couldn't blame them. A respite sounded welcome to her, too.

On this frosty Saturday afternoon, she sat sipping Earl Grey tea at Betty's when the phone rang. Betty answered it, her voice rising in elation as she talked.

Finally hanging up, she exclaimed, "Goodness gracious!" Turning to Elizabeth she continued, "That was Mary Joe, the librarian. They found my Jell-O recipe tucked away in <u>The New Jell-O Book of Surprises</u> that I borrowed! The recipe card is waiting at the library for me."

Betty clasped her hands joyfully. "Now, I can make my famous Jell-O recipe for the Christmas gathering after all. What a relief!"

Elizabeth smiled, knowing how vexed her friend had been over the missing recipe. "I'm so glad they located it for you, Betty. Your party will be a hit now with your signature dessert."

"Bless the library staff for taking the time to find it," Betty replied gratefully. She hurried to fetch her coat and hat. "Let's pop over there right now and collect it before more time slips away!"

Amused by her neighbor's urgency, Elizabeth readily agreed it was worth braving the December chill.

As Elizabeth and Betty walked to the library, they passed the Village Green where folks were stringing lights on the big Christmas tree and assembling the nativity scene. Soon they would add the live animals around the manger tableau before the annual tree lighting.

Arriving at the library, Mary Joe stood waiting with a smile. "I have that missing recipe card all ready for you, Betty!"

Betty hurried over and took the card excitedly. "Oh, bless you, dear, I've been hunting for this for months. My famous Jell-O recipe is back on the menu!"

"We're so glad we could locate it for you," Mary Joe replied. "It was tucked away in the Jell-O book you borrowed."

"Well, thank the Lord for diligent librarians!" Betty declared. "Now I can make my dessert for the Christmas gathering after all."

Elizabeth enjoyed seeing how happy her neighbor was to recover the cherished recipe in time for the holidays. Leaving the library, the scent of fresh pine wafted from the Village Green where more carolers had gathered to decorate the tree.

The recipes, decorations, and carols were all joyful harbingers of the approaching Christmas spirit. With the rediscovered recipe card in hand, Betty and Elizabeth walked home practically humming a cheerful tune under their breath.

The next day, Elizabeth was passing a quiet Sunday afternoon at home when a frantic knocking startled her. She opened the door to a panicked Betty.

"The Japanese! They've bombed Hawaii!" Betty cried breathlessly. "It's all over the radio, come quick!"

Alarmed, they rushed to Betty's house just as a news announcer described how the US Navy fleet at Pearl Harbor had been decimated by Japanese bombers, with only a few ships escaping destruction.

As the terrifying reports continued, another hurried knock came. It was Samuel, who had sped over as soon as he heard.

"How are you ladies holding up?" he asked with deep concern, embracing a shaken Elizabeth.

"We're in utter shock," Elizabeth replied. "Just this morning, all seemed calm. Now, war has reached us."

"The world will never be the same," said Samuel.

Darkness and conflict had engulfed their nation, too. Elizabeth clutched Samuel's hand tightly, afraid, yet resolute. They would stand united to combat tyranny, no matter the tumultuous days ahead.

As night fell, Worthington's future seemed so tenuous. But Elizabeth drew courage knowing she did not stand alone. Linking arms, she and Samuel bid Betty goodnight, their solidarity bolstering their spirits. Whatever tomorrow held, they would face it together.

Feeling the need for company after the devastating news, Elizabeth invited Samuel over, not wanting to be alone on such a painful day.

As dusk fell earlier with the recent daylight savings change, she made a simple dinner of chicken which they ate quietly, the weight of events heavy on their minds.

After tidying up, Samuel offered "Here, let me build us a fire." He neatly stacked kindling in the hearth while Elizabeth poured glasses of sweet red wine. Snowflakes started to come down outside as she pulled down the blinds.

Turning on the radio, they were met with more chilling updates from Pearl Harbor. Elizabeth hastily switched stations from the news until the soft notes of a song called "Ohio Snowfall" were heard playing on the radio.

"Oh, this song is new," Samuel remarked as he settled on the couch next to her, handsome in his sweater. Elizabeth passed him a wine glass and savored a sip, comforted by his presence.

As the mellow music filled the space, the tension of the day dissipated slightly. Curled beside Samuel gazing at the flickering fire, the horrors unfolding outside Worthington's borders felt temporarily at bay.

Today their nation had been attacked, but tonight they took respite in the tranquil scene - snow drifting down, fire crackling, music swirling softly. No matter what lay ahead, they would face it arm in arm.

Curled together as the snow fell softly outside, Elizabeth gazed at Samuel and said "You've brought my world back to life since you returned."

Samuel cradled her face, meeting her eyes. "And you've reawakened life in me, Elizabeth."

They sipped their wine slowly before Samuel leaned in, kissing her deeply as everything else slipped away for a blissful moment. They held onto each other on the couch with Samuel pulling up a warm blanket over them. Eventually, they drifted off by the fire as the snow continued fell gently.

In the morning, Elizabeth awoke to the alarm next to her bed, Samuel had already gone. He must have carried her to her bed at some point in the night.

Getting ready for school, Elizabeth took in the serene snow-covered trees outside. But in class, the children were filled with questions about the attack. Little Amy looked especially downcast. "What happens now?" she asked sadly.

"I don't know sweetheart, I don't know," Elizabeth replied with her head down.

At lunch, the teachers gathered to hear Roosevelt's address to the nation. His fiery words made clear war was imminent. Elizabeth's heart sank, realizing that Samuel was right - the world would never be the same.

Leaving school after classes, she stopped by the bulletin board where notices had been posted about rationing and air raid preparations. Worthington, like the rest of America, was girded for battle.

Elizabeth sighed, her breath a wispy cloud. Dark days lay ahead. But the snow-cloaked calm reminded her that light and hope endured if one just knew where to look for it.

On Friday evening, Elizabeth, Betty, and Samuel joined the village folk on the snow-blanketed Village Green for the annual tree lighting ceremony.

For the first time in years, the ground was frosted white, lending an extra magical air. As Mayor Henderson stood on stage about to light up the Christmas tree, the crowd eagerly counted down.

At the cue, the tree gloriously lit up, eliciting cheers and applause. Nearby, the live nativity scene featured sheep and a donkey gathered around the manger like something from a Christmas card.

Moved by the spirit, someone began singing "O Little Town of Bethlehem" in a clear voice. Soon everyone joyfully joined in, voices rising together under the starry sky.

Afterwards, they broke into smaller groups caroling door to door along the quaint homes edging the green. The holiday songs and generosity of spirit contrasted sharply with the specter of war.

Arm in arm with Samuel, sharing a wrap, Elizabeth felt her heart swell. Despite the darkness looming ahead, this luminous scene was proof that light and hope endured.

Worthington's undaunted streets resounded with melody and camaraderie. Even in trying times, their bonds remained unbroken. This simple yet profound truth lifted Elizabeth's spirit immensely.

On Monday, Elizabeth left school early. She and Betty took a taxi to the Lazarus department store in downtown Columbus to shop for a new dress. Elizabeth felt she needed something to wear since she and Samuel had volunteered to chaperone the high school dance, appropriately called, "The Christmas Crystal Ball".

As they entered the grand emporium, Betty remarked "You know it was Mr. Lazarus who convinced FDR to move Thanksgiving to the third Thursday in November. It gives people more time to prepare for Christmas shopping!"

Elizabeth took in the elaborate holiday decorations adorning the store - wreaths, garlands, ribbons, and bows everywhere. The centerpiece was Santa's Land, a miniature Christmas village with model trains, dolls, elves, and candy canes surrounding a beaming live Santa Claus.

The ladies made their way back towards the women's dress department. Betty stopped and tried on a black fascinator hat that she adored only to say it was too expensive. Elizabeth looked at the dresses and decided to try on some shimmery, festive styles. Finally, Elizabeth emerged from the fitting room in a dress that made Betty gasp.

It was a red satin sheath with cap sleeves, nipped in at the waist then flaring into a full skirt. The sweetheart neckline and faceted buttons ran down the back.

Elizabeth beamed, doing a little twirl. "I feel like a Christmas queen in this one!" Betty heartily agreed it was perfect for the dance.

As Elizabeth admired herself in the mirrors, she imagined dancing in Samuel's arms, the dress swirling around her. The image filled her with warmth and joy.

After purchasing shoes and a matching fur stole, they left laden with packages, Elizabeth giddy with anticipation for the magical night ahead.

That Friday Elizabeth and Samuel arrived at the Christmas Crystal Ball-themed dance at the high school. Elizabeth looked into the gymnasium where the student dance band was tuning up their instruments. Parents were standing on chairs stringing Christmas decorations around the walls. A few parents had gotten a ladder and managed to hang up a glass chandelier on the ceiling and strung it up with rope on the wall.

Samuel looked dapper in his black suit and red and green scarf. "You look lovely in that festive dress." he said.

"And you cut such a dashing figure yourself," Elizabeth smiled. She took his coat so he could offer his arm to escort her inside.

They ladled out cups of punch, the fruity aroma bringing back memories. "Just like old times," Samuel remarked wistfully.

Elizabeth turned around to see Mrs. Collins walking up to her.

"I thought you were with that George guy," she said glaringly to Elizabeth.

"Mrs. Collins, what a nice surprise! How on Earth did you learn that the high school needed chaperones for the dance?"

"Word travels fast, Elizabeth, at the Lady Alice Beauty Salon. Almost as fast as you change men," replied Mrs. Collins.

Elizabeth sarcastically smiled back.

Suddenly the band started playing a peppy tune. "Oh good, they're starting! We'd best get back, excuse us, Mrs. Collins." Elizabeth said. When they went back into the gymnasium, the main lights had been turned off and white lights were aimed up at the chandelier casting a shiny, glittering snowflake effect onto the dance floor.

"It's as if it is a winter wonderland inside," Samuel said smiling.

Students swayed happily to the upbeat big band music. Elizabeth kept her eyes on the exuberant students. Danny waved excitedly as he foxtrotted by with his date.

"Where's your camera, Danny?" Elizabeth jokingly laughed.

"Don't worry Miss Russo, I've got my camera right there." He pointed to a bag sitting on the bleachers. "A photographer is always prepared," Danny assured her. His date just grinned indulgently.

Watching the teenagers twirling around the gym, Elizabeth was transported back to simpler times. The enchanting holiday music and Samuel's familiar embrace filled her heart to the brim. For one night, all cares melted away under the glittering lights.

Towards the end of the night, as the dance progressed, the student band suddenly broke into an upbeat, familiar foxtrot - "Don't Make Your Pappa Sad."

"Remember this song?" Samuel asked excitedly. "From our school dances!" Before she could protest, he whisked Elizabeth onto the dance floor.

At first self-conscious, Elizabeth soon lost herself in the spirited steps just like old times. The students clapped along, clearly impressed by Samuel's smooth moves and Elizabeth's flowing dress. The students soon got out of the way and made a circle around the two.

When the last notes rang out, the whole gymnasium erupted in applause for their performance. Blushing but exhilarated, Elizabeth took a playful bow hand-in-hand with a beaming Samuel.

Suddenly, Samuel looked directly up and shouted, "Look out!" pushing Elizabeth out of the way.

The glass chandelier came crashing down shattering into sharp, jagged pieces on the gymnasium floor. A girl shrieked at the horror. Shards of crystal glass filled the gym but no one was hurt.

"We could have been killed!" Elizabeth said, looking into Samuel's wide brown eyes.

Elizabeth then glanced over to the side to see Mrs. Collins quickly walking away from where the rope had been attached to a pulley holding the chandelier on the ceiling. It now appeared that the rope was frayed and had been intentionally cut loose.

"Mrs. Collins did that!" Elizabeth angrily said to Samuel as she pointed to the woman hastily exiting the gymnasium.

"Did you see her do it?" asked Samuel.

"No, but I know she did it," Elizabeth said, still upset.

"Look, we're alright Lizzy and none of the students are hurt. If you didn't see her mess with the rope then we don't have solid proof," said Samuel taking her hand. "It's time to call it a night anyways, sweetheart."

Samuel and Elizabeth wished everyone a good night and helped clean up the floor. As the remaining shocked students and parents walked out, there stood Mrs. Collins waiting for them outside.

"Things were going great until they came to a crashing halt." Mrs. Collins slyly grinned.

"You did that on purpose, Mrs. Collins!" Elizabeth yelled.

"Now, now Lizzy, let's get back home," said Samuel as he opened the door and beckoned Elizabeth into the car. Elizabeth angrily got in the passenger seat.

Samuel drove Elizabeth home in silence. He got out to open the car door for her under the cold winter moonlight. "So, I'll see you tomorrow evening at Betty's Christmas party?" he asked hopefully.

Elizabeth, still angry "Yes, at least I don't have to worry about a chandelier falling on me over there," she said with a sarcastic smile.

Samuel smiled back and said, "No, you just have to watch out for the Jell-O."

The two laughed. As he grew closer to her, he leaned in, holding her hand.

He whispered, "You know Elizabeth, I know the last few months have been hard on you but it also feels like magic that we've found each other again."

Elizabeth felt a magnetic pull towards him. She whispered back, "We have to believe we are magic."

He kissed her sweetly, the two embracing the magical moment, wishing it would never end.

Elizabeth stepped out of the car. Waving goodbye, and considering that most of the night was a wonderful ball, she practically floated up her front steps. The evening had been magical - a chance to cut loose and recapture their youthful joy, even if the chandelier may have been cut loose too. She retired for the night letting go of any anger, reminiscing about the night with her special guy.

Chapter 13: A Towering Holiday Party

As soon as school got out Elizabeth rushed home. The holiday break was to begin the following afternoon. Elizabeth arrived at Betty's to help her prepare for the Christmas party, even though it would just be the three of them.

"My, this is a feast!" Elizabeth remarked, eyeing the heaping platters of turkey, casseroles and of course, Betty's famous Jell-O dessert.

"Nonsense, you two are my dearest friends, practically family. You deserve a holiday banquet!" Betty tutted.

Elizabeth smiled. "Well, since it's just us, I want you to open your gift now." She handed Betty a neatly wrapped box.

Unwrapping it eagerly, Betty gasped when she saw the black fascinator hat from Lazarus she had admired. "How on Earth did you sneak this without me noticing?" she exclaimed.

"I had Samuel pick it up for me," Elizabeth admitted. "I knew you had to have it."

Betty gave her a fierce hug. "You darling girl!" Elizabeth was glad to see Betty so delighted.

It was getting dark out and soon Samuel arrived. "Sorry I'm late ladies, the snow is really picking up out there," he said, stomping the slush off his boots. "They say we're getting blizzard conditions."

"Well hurry inside where it's warm!" Betty exclaimed. The wind howled outside as if to emphasize her point.

Once Samuel had removed his snow-dusted outerwear, they settled in the parlor where a fire crackled cheerily against the storm brewing outside.

"My, Betty, what a hearty spread, and I adore that lovely hat." Samuel said, admiring the work that Betty had put into the feast.

"Thank you, Samuel. Elizabeth got me this hat. I adore it!" replied Betty.

As the snow came down, the real joy was in their warm company on this special night. Gazing around the table, Elizabeth's heart brimmed with gratitude. This was the true gift of the season.

Samuel asked, "So what's the secret behind this famous Jell-O dessert, Betty? It looks like lemon chiffon pie."

"Oh, it's quite simple really," she explained. "It's called, Paradise Pudding. I got the recipe from People's Home Journal. It is lemon Jell-O, almonds, marshmallows, macaroons and whipped cream. Then I place maraschino cherries on top!"

"It looks so magical and delicious!" Elizabeth said.

Slicing the Paradise Pudding, whose layers glistened festively, Betty poured eggnog. "A toast to friends!" she proclaimed, lifting her glass.

"To friends," Elizabeth and Samuel echoed, clinking their glasses. Nothing could ruin this snug scene filled with love, laughter and the sweetness of Betty's dessert. The blizzard only seemed to make their camaraderie cozier.

After admiring her new hat, Betty called, "Come now, let's eat before the food gets cold."

Just then a loud knock made them jump.

"Who could that be in this sort of weather?" questioned Betty.

Samuel opened the door, but it was only the wind howling outside as the blizzard raged on.

"Goodness, what a fright!" Betty said. "I thought for a moment it was carolers out in this mess."

"It must have just been the wind," said Samuel, looking out at the downpour of snow.

But then a dark figure lunged out from beside the door, knocking Samuel down. It was a wild-eyed Dr. Bentley, clutching a knife.

"Merry Christmas!" he cried maniacally, pinning Samuel and raising the blade.

Thinking fast, Betty seized the urn holding her late husband's ashes on the fireplace mantel, rushed over to Dr. Bentley, and cracked it over his head. "Take that, you fiend!"

"Ouch! Damn you all!" cried Dr. Bentley now covered in ash.

With the front door still open, Bentley reeled from the blow. Samuel kicked the dropped knife onto the snowy ground outside. "Elizabeth, the cooking pan!" he yelled.

Elizabeth dumped the green beans from the pan onto the floor. Then tossed the pan to Samuel. As Bentley lunged for the knife again, Samuel raised the pan to block him. Seizing the weapon, Bentley turned and fled into the snowy night.

"After him!" Samuel shouted. Betty grabbed another pan and tossed it to Elizabeth.

"I'll call for help!" said Betty.

"Thanks, Betty!" yelled Elizabeth as she took off running up New England Avenue as Samuel pursued Bentley.

The snow blew in blinding sheets as they struggled to keep the dark figure in sight. Passing a cheery party at the slanted Snow House across from the New England Inn, Samuel yelled, "Call the police!" as an on-looker walked to the house.

Elizabeth slipped and slid trying to keep up as the men's footprints rapidly vanished ahead. Pressing forward against the stinging wind, she found Bentley running on the sidewalk, the knife still in hand. Samuel was racing towards him, pan still raised warily.

"It's over, Bentley!" he panted. "No more running." The doctor just groaned and kept running.

As Dr. Bentley fled into the blizzard, Samuel spotted him sprinting past the New England Inn and across High Street, nearly getting hit by a passing car. Patrons at the inn walked outside gasping in shock.

"Call the police!" Samuel shouted as he and Elizabeth took off in pursuit, her waving the pan wildly. They repeated the plea to the stunned onlookers.

The chase continued up High Street, weaving around startled pedestrians. Dr. Bentley, with the knife in hand, dashed by the Lady Alice Salon, with Jane emerging outside in shock.

"What's happening?" Jane cried as Elizabeth yelled "Get the police!" without slowing.

At the Red and White store, John walked out to see the commotion. He displayed a look of shock as the bizarre scene careened by. "Call for help, John!" Elizabeth implored breathlessly waiving the pan in her hands.

She could see Bentley angling towards the water tower now. "He's headed for the tower!" she shouted to Samuel. Her lungs burned from the freezing air.

Reaching the tower's shadow, they discovered Dr. Bentley trying to scale the rungs. But he had only made it part way up the icy ladder.

"Enough, Bentley!" Samuel demanded. "There's nowhere left to run. Give up!"

TRAPPED, DR. BENTLEY glared down at them panting but he kept on climbing up the ladder. The sound was nearly drowned out by the wind. Gripping the icy rungs, Dr. Bentley ascended higher as Samuel climbed determinedly after him. Looking up at the towering water tank, Elizabeth steeled her nerves.

"The things I do for love," she muttered, placing her belt around her panhandle. She then began to follow them up the treacherous ladder.

The freezing metal numbed Elizabeth's hands as the winter wind buffeted her. Looking up, Samuel was barely visible through the thickly falling snow.

Another blast of air nearly blew Elizabeth off the ladder. She clung on desperately, hands cramping, but continued upwards.

Finally, she hauled herself onto the platform at the top. Samuel was walking towards Bentley, who stood back against the railings still with the knife in hand.

"Let's talk about this reasonably," Samuel urged holding the pan up over the gale.

Bentley's eyes darted wildly for an escape. Inching closer, Samuel said gently, "It's over. Ease your conscience and end this peacefully."

Seeing Bentley's despairing look, Elizabeth now on the platform, felt only pity for the broken man. His reign of shadows had ended.

As the blizzard swirled violently atop the tower, a crazed Bentley cried "You've ruined everything! We were so close to the insurance money and escaping to California. Now you'll pay the price for your meddling!"

He charged at Samuel with the knife raised. "Get back, Elizabeth!" Samuel warned, bracing with his pot lid.

Suddenly a shot cracked through the howling wind. Bentley's eyes went wide before he toppled over the railing, out of sight. Elizabeth gasped - behind where he'd stood was Mrs. Collins, holding a smoking pistol.

The screech of tires on icy pavement rose from below. Squad cars and an ambulance with flashing lights ringed the tower base.

"He never could get anything done right," she muttered coldly. Turning the gun on Samuel, she hissed "But I always handle matters correctly. No mistakes this time."

Elizabeth and Samuel stood paralyzed. Just as Mrs. Collins' finger tightened on the trigger, a small voice pierced the night. "Mommy, don't!"

Far below, little Amy in her pajamas clutched her teddy bear, surrounded by a crowd. Mrs. Collins faltered, anguish crossing her face.

"Mrs. Collins," Samuel spoke gently, edging closer. "It's over now. It's okay, now let go of the gun."

Tears welling in her eyes, Mrs. Collins finally lowered the shaking gun. Samuel gripped the barrel and she released it into his hands.

Just then Officer Jameson could be heard talking on his police cruiser loudspeaker. "Come on folks, let's get down from this infernal tower before we all freeze to death!"

Descending the ladder, Elizabeth glimpsed Bentley's motionless body being covered by a tarp - a sad fate for a corrupted soul. But as she reunited with Samuel and Betty below, joy replaced sorrow. The light had triumphed over the darkness that night.

Safely on the ground again, Officer Jameson moved to arrest Mrs. Collins. "Ma'am, you're under arrest for the murder of Dr. Bentley."

But then from the shadows, Detective Morris from the sheriff's office and Worthington Police Chief Engel stepped forward.

Detective Morris turned to Elizabeth. "That camera film of yours that Danny from the high school provided us cracked this case wide open. We've been building evidence against these snakes for some time now. Unfortunately, they lashed out before we could make an arrest. Thank you, Miss Russo, for all your help."

Mrs. Collins was led away in handcuffs. Elizabeth turned to Samuel in weary relief. "It's finally over. The long nightmare is finally over."

Betty walked over to the two and drew them both into a big hug. "We sure lit a candle against all that darkness. But good won in the end, as I knew it would all along!"

With the culprit bundled into a police car and Dr. Bentley's body being removed, Elizabeth suddenly cried, "But what about Amy?"

The detective tipped his hat reassuringly. "Not to worry ma'am, the girl's coming with me."

Samuel took Elizabeth's hand. "And dinner's getting cold back at Betty's."

Trudging through the deepening snow, they returned to Betty's cozy house, though Harold's ashes were still scattered about from the urn breaking.

"Oh dear, I'm so sorry Betty," Samuel said ruefully as he helped tidy up.

But Betty just laughed heartily. "Are you kidding? Harold would've loved seeing some good fight. Nothing merrier than a brawl before Christmas!"

Soon they were gathered around the feast, now cooled but still delicious. Raising his wine glass, Samuel proclaimed, "To dear friends and solving mysteries!"

They clinked their glasses, camaraderie warming them more than any fire could. The cold blizzard continued relentlessly outside, but within those walls, all was snug and bright.

Elizabeth gazed around at the twinkling lights on the tree, the remains of their meal, and Betty humming carols while she freshened up the cocoa. Here, on this holy night, was everything worth fighting for - not riches or schemes, but love, faith, and fellowship with those who light our way through the shadows.

After bidding Betty goodnight, Elizabeth and Samuel trudged through the deepening snow to her place.

"Just stay here tonight. I don't want to be alone," Elizabeth implored, still shaken by the harrowing ordeal. Samuel readily agreed.

In his comforting embrace, she finally slept peacefully. The next morning, he dropped her off at school, thoughts still with little Amy and her uncertain future.

At lunchtime, as the students excitedly left, a knock surprised Elizabeth. It was Detective Morris. "I just wanted to properly thank you for your critical help on this case," he said.

Elizabeth smiled. "Does this mean Mrs. Collins confessed everything?"

"She did - framing the vagrant, the involvement in killing her husband, Dr. Bentley killing Milkman Bailey and trying to bribe Officer Jameson." The detective shook his head. "Without you, the truth may never have come to light."

But why didn't you arrest him sooner?"

Morris sighed. "We lacked hard evidence. Officer Jameson was working undercover, trying to gather information. His 'gambling debts' were part of his cover."

Elizabeth's brow furrowed. "But why would Dr. Bentley just show up at Betty's and try to kill us?"

"Ah, that's the tragic part," Morris explained. "Earlier in the evening, Dr. Bentley and Mrs. Collins had a violent argument. In a drunken rage, he attempted to kill her but failed. Realizing his plans were unraveling, he decided to take his anger out on you folks. He knew it was over for him."

Elizabeth shuddered, remembering the wild look in Bentley's eyes.

"We couldn't risk tipping our hand until we had solid evidence," Morris confirmed.

"Well, I'm just glad it's all over," Samuel said, putting an arm around Elizabeth.

Morris nodded. "Thanks to you, Miss Russo, the truth finally came to light. Worthington owes you a debt of gratitude."

Elizabeth had mixed feelings of relief and lingering shock. "It seems there were even more layers to this mystery than we realized," she mused.

Elizabeth eagerly asked, "Has Jeff been released then?"

"Not yet, but I'm headed there now, as soon as the judge signs off. Would you like to join me in informing him?"

Elizabeth readily agreed. Principal Gentry happily took over her class, with him waving her off encouragingly.

At the jail, the guard led Elizabeth and the detective to a small room. Minutes later, a bewildered Jeff was ushered inside.

Overcome with emotion, Elizabeth cried "You're free, Jeff! It's over. Mrs. Collins confessed to everything."

Disbelief, then elation washed over Jeff's newly shaven, weathered face. He turned to the detective who handed him discharge forms. "You're cleared of all charges, sir. Our apologies for the mistakes," said Detective Morris.

Jeff shook the man's hand vigorously before embracing a joyful Elizabeth. As they walked outside, she imagined his future now full of possibility and light.

Detective Morris drove Elizabeth and Jeff back to Worthington, outside his humble shack near the rail yard. "I don't know how to repay your kindness, ma'am," Jeff said humbly.

Elizabeth smiled. "Well, you've cleaned yourself up nicely. Perhaps I could help you find steadier work - at the Red and White Store."

Jeff tipped his worn cap. "God bless you, Miss Russo. You've given me back my life."

As they continued into the village, gentlemen tipped their hats to Elizabeth in thanks. "They know you were the one to help uncover the truth," Detective Morris said.

Elizabeth just blushed, unaccustomed to such recognition. Dropping her off and bidding the detective farewell, she went inside her quiet home, looking forward to some peace.

Worthington was healing, emerging from darkness. They had not let evil prevail over good. Though shadows inevitably came, love shone all the brighter against that contrast. Tonight, all was calm, all was bright.

Soon Christmas arrived in Worthington. On that day, Elizabeth was relaxing at home when the phone rang. It was her mother calling from Cincinnati to wish her a Merry Christmas and to chat about her busy social calendar.

Elizabeth smiled indulgently, though inwardly longing for a simpler life. After begging off her mother's New Year's Eve Party invitation, a knock came at the door. It was Samuel with a bouquet.

"Merry Christmas, my darling!" he beamed, stomping the snow off his boots before entering. Elizabeth welcomed him in, simply content in his company.

Another knock soon followed. A man in a dark suit stood there. He said, "Good day ma'am, my name is Lance Hawkins. I'm the attorney for Mrs. Collins. She wanted you to have this," handing Elizabeth a letter.

Elizabeth gasped as she read Mrs. Collins' request for her to care for little Amy since she had no other family left. Before she could respond, Amy herself bounded up the steps.

"Mommy said I get to live with you!" she cried joyfully, hugging Elizabeth with her teddy bear tucked under one arm.

Elizabeth turned to Samuel in shock. But he just smiled warmly. "Well, why don't you invite her in? It is Christmas after all."

As Amy came in, she gleefully shook a snow globe on the kitchen table. Elizabeth felt both deeply moved and overwhelmed by the sudden responsibility.

Seeing her expression, Samuel squeezed her hand supportively. "We'll figure this out together," he said. Elizabeth exhaled, knowing with him by her side, she could face any challenge.

Though life was far from settled, on this Christmas day, love and hope had been renewed. The future seemed bright as the two of them watched Amy play happily by the fire, at last sheltered and in peace.

After all, there was no more underlying love, it had now reached the surface on full display.

The End

Don't miss out!

Visit the website below and you can sign up to receive emails whenever Bradley Barkhurst publishes a new book. There's no charge and no obligation.

https://books2read.com/r/B-A-MWKJB-YCWID

BOOKS2READ

Connecting independent readers to independent writers.

Also by Bradley Barkhurst

The AI Handbook
The AI Handbook: A Practical Guide for Non-Experts

Underlying Love
Underlying Love A Worthington, Ohio Mystery

About the Author

Bradley Barkhurst grew up in Worthington, Ohio, and graduated from Thomas Worthington High School in 1995. He is a graduate of the University of Cincinnati with a BFA in Electronic Media. After graduating, he worked as a TV producer in Cincinnati, Ohio. Since 2006, he has worked in digital forensics specializing in audio/video forensics. In 2020, he obtained an MSc in Digital Investigation and Forensic Computing from the University College of Dublin, Ireland. In 2023, he took a class on AI and business from MIT. This book resulted from Bradley's desire to create a product using AI.